I0651298

Frederick W. Robinson

Mattie

a stray - Vol. 3

Frederick W. Robinson

Mattie
a stray - Vol. 3

ISBN/EAN: 9783337276829

Printed in Europe, USA, Canada, Australia, Japan

Cover: Foto ©Andreas Hilbeck / pixelio.de

More available books at **www.hansebooks.com**

MATTIE:—A STRAY.

BY

THE AUTHOR OF

"HIGH CHURCH," "NO CHURCH,"
"OWEN:—A WAIF,"
&c., &c.

"By bestowing blessings upon others, we entail them on ourselves."
HORACE SMITH.

IN THREE VOLUMES.

VOL. III.

LONDON:
HURST AND BLACKETT, PUBLISHERS,
SUCCESSORS TO HENRY COLBURN,
13, GREAT MARLBOROUGH STREET
1864.

CONTENTS

OF

THE THIRD VOLUME.

BOOK VI.

SIDNEY'S FRIENDS.

BOOK VII.

SIDNEY'S GRATITUDE.

BOOK VIII.

MORE LIGHT.

BOOK VI.

SIDNEY'S FRIENDS.

MATTIE: A STRAY.

CHAPTER I.

MATTIE'S CHOICE.

THERE are epochs in some lives when the heart cracks or hardens. When humanity, wrung to its utmost, gives way, or ossifies. Both are dangerous crises, and require more than ordinary care; the physician must be skilful and understand human nature, or his efforts at cure will only kill the patient who submits to his remedies.

Man—we speak literally of the masculine gender at this point—though born unto trouble, finds it hard to support in a philosophical

B 2

way. A great trouble that in nine cases out of ten
shows woman at her best, transforms man to his
worst; if he be a man of the world, worldly, he
is dumbfounded by the calamity which has fallen
upon him. It is incomprehensible why *he* should
suffer—he of all men—and 'he wraps himself in
his egotism—his wounded self-love—and thinks of
the injustice and hardness that have shut him out
from his labours.

Such men, heavily oppressed, do not give in to
the axiom, that it is well for them to be afflicted;
they will not bow to God's will, or resign themselves to it—their outward calmness is assumed, and they chafe at the Great Hand which
has arrested them midway. Such men will turn
misanthropes and atheists, at times.

Sidney Hinchford after all was a man of the
world. In the world he had lived and fought upwards. There had been a charm in making his
way in it, and the obstacles ahead had but
nerved his arm to resist, and his heart to endure.
He had talents for success in the commercial world
—even a genius for making money. With time

before him, possibly Sidney Hinchford would have risen to greatness.

To make money—and to keep it when made—requires as much genius as to make poetry, rather more, perhaps. A genius of a different order, but a very fine one notwithstanding, and one which we can admire at a distance—on the kerb stones with our manuscripts under our arms, waiting for the genius's carriage to pass, before we cross to our publishers'. Is not that man a genius who in these latter days rises to wealth by his own exertions, in lieu of having wealth thrust upon him? A genius, with wondrous powers of discrimination, not to be led into a bad thing, but seeing before other people the advantages to accrue from a good one, and making his investments accordingly. A man who peers into the future and beholds his own advancement, not the step before him, but the apex in the clouds, lost to less keen-sighted folk fighting away at the base—therefore, a wonderful man.

We believe that Sidney Hinchford, like his uncle before him, would have risen in the world; he believed it also, and throughout his past career—

though we have seen him anxious—he never lost
his hope of ultimate success.   When he knew that
there must come a period of tribulation and darkness for him, he had trusted to have time left him
for position ; and not till time was denied him, and
the darkness set in suddenly, did he give up the
battle.   And then he did not give way ; he hardened.

Sidney had never been a religious man, therefore he sought no consolation in his affliction, and
believed not in the power of religion to console. He
had been pure-minded, honourable, earnest, everything that makes the good worldly man, but he
had never been grateful to God for his endow-
ments, and he bore God's affliction badly in consequence.   He felt balked in his endeavour to
prosper, therefore, aggrieved, and the darkness that
had stolen over his senses seemed to find its way to
his heart and transform him.

The clergyman, who had attended his father,
attempted consolation with him, but he would have
" none of it."   He did not complain, he said ; he
had faced the worst—it was with him, and there was

an end of it. Do not weary him with trite bible-
texts, but leave him to himself.

And by himself he sat down to brood over the
inevitable wrong that had been done him; he,
in the vigour of life and thought, shut apart from
action! Once he had looked forward to a
consolation even in distress, but that was to have
been a long day hence. Now his day had been
shortened, and the consolation was denied him.
He knew that *that* was lost, and he had thought of
a fight with the world to benumb the thoughts of the
future; and then the world was shut away from him
also, and he was broken down, inactive and lost.

He and his uncle were the only attendants
at the funeral; he was informed afterwards 'that
Mattie had stood at the grave's edge, and seen the
last of her old friend and first patron; then his
uncle had left him, failing in all efforts to console him. Geoffry Hinchford offered his nephew
money, all the influence at his disposal in any way
or shape, but Sidney declined all coldly. He
did not require help yet awhile, he had saved
money; he preferred being left to himself in that

desolate home; presently, when he had grown reconciled to these changes, he should find courage
to think what was best; meanwhile, those who
loved him—he even told Mattie that—would leave
him to himself.

Mattie made no effort to intrude upon him in
the early days following the double loss; she was
perplexed as to her future course, her method of
fulfilling that promise made to Sidney's father on
his death-bed. Her common sense assured her
that in the first moments of sorrow, intrusion
would be not only unavailing, but irritating—and
her belief in becoming of service to Sidney was
but a small one at the best. In the good, far-away
time she might be a humble agent in bringing
Harriet Wesden and him together; Harriet who
must love him out of very pity now, and forget
that wounded pride which had followed the annul-
ment of engagement.

Meanwhile, she remained quiet and watchful;
busy at her dress-making, busy in her father's
home, attentive to that new father whom she had
found, and who was very kind to her, though he

scarcely seemed to understand her. Still, they
agreed well together, for Mattie was submissive,
and Mr. Gray had more than a fair share of his
own way; and he was a man who liked his own
way, and with whom it agreed vastly. But we
have seen that he was a jealous man, and that
Mattie's interest in Mr. Wesden had discomfited
him. He was a good man we know, but jealousy
got the upper hand of him at times, when he was
scarcely aware of it himself, for he attributed his
excitement, perhaps his envy, to very different
feelings. He was even jealous of a local preacher
of his own denomination, a man who had made a
convert of a most vicious article—an article that
he had been seeking all his life, and had never
found in full perfection.

Mr. Gray over his work said little concerning
Ann Packet's occasional visits to his domicile, but
he objected to them notwithstanding, for they
drew his daughter's attention away from himself.
He liked still less Mattie's visits to Chesterfield
Terrace—flying visits, when she saw Ann Packet
for an hour and Sidney Hinchford for a minute,

looking in at the last moment, and heralded by Ann exclaiming,

"Here's Mattie come to see you, sir."

"Ah, Mattie!" Sid would answer, turning his face towards the door whence the voice issued, and attempting the feeblest of smiles.

"Is there anything that I can do, sir, for you?"

"No, girl, thank you."

He would quickly relapse into that thought again, from which her presence had aroused him —and it was a depth of thought upon which the fugitive efforts of Mattie had no effect. Standing in the shadowy doorway she would watch him for awhile, then draw the door to after her and go away grieving at the change in him.

The thought occurred to her that Harriet Wesden might even at that early stage work some amount of good until she heard from Ann Packet that Harriet and her father had called one day, and that Sidney had refused an interview. He was unwell; some other day when he was better; it was kind to call, but he could not be seen then, had been his excuses sent out by the servant maid. Mattie, who had always found time do good, and work many changes, left the result to time, until honest Ann one evening, when Mr. Gray was at work at his old post, asserted her fears that Sidney was getting worse instead of better.

" I think he'll go melancholic mad like, poor dear," she said; "and it's no good my trying to brighten him a bit—he's wus at that, which is nat'ral, not being in my line, and wanting brightening up myself. He does nothing but brood, brood, brood, sitting of a heap all day in that chair!"

" A month since his father died now," said Mattie, musing.

" To the very day, Mattie."

" He goes to church—you read the Bible to him?" asked Mr. Gray, suddenly.

" He can't go by hisself—he's not very handy with his blindness, like those who have been brought up to it with a dog and a tin mug," said Ann in reply ; "but let's hope he'll get used to it, and find it a comfort to him, sir."

" I asked you also, young woman, if you ever read the Bible to him ?"

" Lor bless you, sir ! I can't read fit enough for him—I take a blessed lot of spelling with it, and it aggravates him. All the larning I've ever had, has come from this dear gal of ours, and *he* taught her first of all !"

" I think that I could do this young man good," said Mr. Gray, suddenly ; " I might impress him with the force of the truth—*convert him.*"

" I would not attempt to preach to him yet," suggested Mattie ; " besides, his is a strange character—you will never understand it."

" You cannot tell what I may be able to understand," he replied, " and I see that my duty lies in that direction. I have been seeking amongst the poor and wretched for a convert, and perhaps it is nearer home—your friend ! "

" I would not worry him in his distress," suggested Mattie anew.

" Worry him !—Mattie, you shock me ! Where's my Bible ?—I'll go at once !"

" We've got Bibles in the house, sir—we're not

cannibals," snapped Ann. Cannibals and heathens were of the same species to Ann Packet.

" Come on, then !"

Mattie half rose, as if with the intention of accompanying her father, but he checked the movement.

"I hope you will remain at home to-night, Mattie," he said; " I never like the house entirely left. It's not business."

Mattie sat down again. She was fidgety at the result of this impromptu movement on her father's part, but saw no way to hinder it. Her father was a man who meant well, but well-meaning men would not do for Sidney Hinchford. Sidney had been well educated; his father was self-taught, and brusque, and Sidney had grown very irritable. In her own little conceited heart she believed that no one could manage Sidney Hinchford save herself Late in the evening, Mr. Gray returned in excellent spirits, rubbing one hand over the other complacently. He had found a new specimen worthy of his powers of conversion.

" Have you seen him ?" asked Mattie.

"To be sure—I went to see him, and he could not keep me out of the room, if I chose to enter. An obstinate young man—as obstinate a young man as I ever remember to have met with in all my life!"

"Did he speak to you?"

"Only twice, once to ask how you were. The second time to tell me that he did not require any preaching to. After that, I read the Bible to him for an hour, locking the door first, to make sure that he did not run for it, blind as he was. Then I gave him the best advice in my power, bade him good night, and came away. He is as hard as the nether millstone ; it will be a glorious victory over the devil to touch his heart and soften it!"

"You are going the wrong way to work. You do not know him!"

"My dear, I know that he's a miserable sinner."

Mattie said no more on the question ; she was not a good hand at argument. At argument, sword's point to sword's point, possibly Mr. Gray would have beaten most men; his ideas were always in order, and he could pounce upon the right word, reason, or text, in an instant; but Mattie was certain that her father's zeal very often outran his discretion. She shuddered as she pictured Sidney Hinchford a victim to her father's obtrusiveness— her father, oblivious to suffering, and full of belief in the conversion he was attempting. She knew that her father was wrong, and she felt vexed that Sidney had been intruded upon at a time wherein she had not found the courage to face him herself. Things must be altered, and her promise to Sid's father must not become a dead letter. In all the world her heart told her she loved Sidney Hinchford best, and that she could make any sacrifice for his sake; and yet Sidney was not getting better, but worse, and her own father would make her hateful to him. The next evening, Mr. Gray came home later than usual. He had been sent for by his employers, had received their commissions, and then, fraught with his new idea, had started for Chesterfield Terrace, to strike a second moral blow at his new specimen.

He came home late, as we have intimated, and began arranging his chimney ornaments, and putting things a little straight, in his usual nervous fashion.

"Mattie, I shall have a job with that young man. He has forbidden me the house; he actually—actually swore at me this evening, for praying for his better heart and moral regeneration."

Mattie compressed her lips, and looked thoughtfully before her for a while. Then the dark eyes turned suddenly and unflinchingly upon her father.

"I have been thinking lately that if I were with him in that house—I, who know him so well—I might do much good."

"You, Mattie!—you?"

"He is without a friend in the world. I knew his father, who was my first friend, and I feel that I am neglecting the son."

"You call there often enough, goodness knows!" Mr. Gray said, a little sharply.

"He is alone—he is blind. What are a few minutes in a long day to him?"

"All this is very ridiculous, Mattie—speaks well for your kind heart, and so on, but, of course, can't be——"

" Of course, must be !"

Mattie had a will of her own when it was needed. A little did not disturb her, but a great deal of opposition could never shake that will when once made up. She had resolved upon her next step, and would proceed with it ; we do not say that she was in the right; we will not profess to constitute her a model heroine in the sight of our readers, who have had enough of model heroines for awhile, and may accept our stray for a change. We are even inclined to believe that Mattie was, in this instance, just a little in the wrong—but then her early training had been defective, and allowance must be made for it. All the evil seeds that neglect has sown in the soil are never entirely eradicated—ask the farmers of land, and the *farmers of souls.*

"Must be !" repeated Mr. Gray, looking in a dreamy manner at his daughter.

" I promised his father to think of him—to study him by all the means in my power. I see that no one understands him but me, and I hear that he is sinking away from all that made him good and noble. I will do my best for him, and there is no one who can stop me here."

" Your father !"

"—Is a new friend, who has been kind to me, and whom I love—but he hasn't the power to make me break my promise to the dead. That man is desolate, and heavily afflicted, and I will go to him !"

" Against MY wish ?"

" Yes—against the wishes of all in the world— if they were uttered in opposition to me !" cried Mattie.

" Then," looking very firm and white, " you will choose between him and me. He will be a friend the more, and I a daughter the less."

" It cannot be helped."

" You never loved me, or you would never thus defy me. Girl, you are going into danger—the world will talk, and rob you of your good name."

" Let it," said Mattie, proudly. " It has spoken ill before of me, and I have lived it down. I shall not study it, when the interest and happiness of a dear friend are at stake. He is being killed by all you!" she cried, with a comprehensive gesture of her hand; "now let me try!"

" Mattie, you are mad—wrong—wicked!—I have no patience with you—I have done with you, if you defy me thus."

" I am doing right—you cannot stop me. I have done wrong to remain idle here so long; I will go at once."

" At once!—breaking up this home—you will, then?"

"If I remain here longer, you will set him against me—me, who would have him look upon me as his sister, his one friend left to pray for him, slave for him, and keep his enemies away!"

" I won't hear any more of this rhodomontade—this voice of the devil on the lips of my child," he said, snatching up his hat again. "Stay here till I return, or go away for ever."

Mr. Gray was in a passion, and, like most men in a passion, went the wrong way to work. He was jealous of this new rival to his daughter's love

that had sprung up, and angered with Mattie's
attempt· to justify her new determination. He
believed in Mattie's obedience, and his own power
over her yet; and he was an obstinate man, whom
it took a long while to subdue. He went out of
the room wildly gesticulating, and Mattie sat pant-
ing for awhile, and trying to still the heaving of
her bosom. She had gone beyond herself—perhaps betrayed herself—but she had expressed her
intention, and nothing that had happened since
had induced her to swerve. If it were a choice
between her father and Sidney, why, it must be
Sidney, if he would have her for his friend and
companion in the future.

"I must go—I must go at once!" she whispered
to herself; and then hurriedly put on her bonnet
and shawl, and made for the staircase. She thought
that she was doing right, and that good would
come of it; and she did not hesitate. Before her,
in the distance, sat the solitary figure of him she
loved, friendless, alone, and benighted; and her
woman's heart yearned to go to him, and forgot
all else.

Thus forgetting, thus yearning to do good, Mattie made a false step, and turned her back upon her father's home.

CHAPTER II.

MATTIE'S ADVISER.

MATTIE reached Chesterfield Terrace as the clock was striking nine. Ann Packet almost shouted with alarm at the sight of the new visitor, and then looked intently over Mattie's shoulder.

" *He* hasn't come back again, has he? Mr. Sidney's been in such a drefful way about him, Mattie. Blind as he is, I think he'll try to murder him."

" I have come instead. He will see me, I hope."

She did not wait to be announced, but turned the handle of the parlour-door and entered. Sidney Hinchford, in a harsh voice, cried out,

" Who's there ?"

" Only Mattie. May I come in ?"

"Mattie here at this hour! Come in, if you will. What is it?"

He was seated in the great leathern arm-chair, that had been his father's favourite seat, in the old attitude that Mattie knew so well now. She shuddered at the change in him—the wreck of manhood that one affliction had reduced him to, and the impulse that had brought her there was strengthened.

"Mr. Sidney," she said, approaching, "I have come to ask a favour of you."

"I am past dispensing favours, Mattie. Unless —unless it's to listen patiently to that horrible father of yours. Then I say No—for he drives me mad with his monotony."

"I have come to defend you from him, if he call again—to live here, and take care of you as a dear brother who requires care, and must not be left entirely to strangers."

"I am better by myself, Mattie—fit company only for myself."

"No, the worst of company for that."

"It must not be."

"I can earn my own living; I shall be no burden to you; I have a hope—such a grand hope, sir!—of making this home a different place to you. Why, I can always make the best of it, I think —*he* thought so, too, before he died."

"Who—my father?" asked Sidney, wondering.

"Yes—he wished that I should come here, and I promised him.   Oh! Mr. Sidney, for a little while, before you have become resigned to this great trouble, let me stay!"

He might have read the truth—the whole truth —in that urgent pleading, but he was shut away from light, and sceptical of any love for him abiding anywhere throughout the world.

"If he wished it, Mattie—stay.   If your father says not No to this, why, stay until you tire of me, and the utter wretchedness of such a life as mine."

"Why utterly wretched?"

"I don't know—don't ask again."

"Others have been afflicted like you before, sir, and borne their heavy burden well."

"Why do you 'sir' me ?   That's new."

"I called your father sir,—you take your father's place," said Mattie, hastily.

"A strange reason—I wonder if it's true."

Mattie coloured, but he could not see her blushes, and whether true or false, mattered little to him then. A new suspicion seized him after awhile, when he had thought more deeply of Mattie's presence there.

"If this is a new trick of your father's to preach to me through you, I warn you, Mattie."

"I have told you why I am here."

"No other reason but that promise to my father?"

"Yes, one promise more—to myself. Mr. Hinchford," she said, noticing his sudden start, "I promised my heart, when I was very young—when I was a stray!—that it should never swerve from those who had befriended me. It will not—it beats the faster with the hope of doing service to all who helped me in my wilful girlhood."

"I told a lie, and said you did not steal my brooch!"

"That was not all, but that taught me gratitude.

Say a lie, but it was a lie that saved me from the prison—from the new life, worse, a thousand times worse than the first."

"You are a strange girl—you were always strange. I am curious to know how soon you will tire of me, or I shall tire of you and this new freak. When I confess you weary me—you will go?"

"Yes."

"Then stay—and God help you with your charge."

His lip curled again, but it was with an effort. He was no true stoic, and Mattie's earnestness had moved him more than he cared to evince. He was curious to note the effect of Mattie's efforts to make the dull world anything better than it was—he who knew how simple-minded and ingenuous Mattie was, and how little she could fathom his thoughts, or understand them. He had spent a month of horrible isolation, and it had seemed long years to him—years in which he had aged and grown grey perhaps, it was more likely than not. He felt like an old man, with whom the world was

a weary resting-place; and he was despondent
enough to wish to die, and end the tragedy that
had befallen him. He had not believed in any
sacrifice for his sake, and Mattie had surprised him
by stealing in upon his solitude, and offering her
help. He was more surprised to think that he had
accepted her services in lieu of turning contemptu-
ously away. It was something new to think of, and
it did him good.

The next day life began anew under Mattie's
supervision. She was the old Mattie of Great
Suffolk Street days—a brisk step and a cheerful
voice, an air of bustle and business about her,
which it was pleasant to hear in the distance.
When the house duties were arranged for the day,
Mattie began her needlework in the parlour where
Sidney sat; and though Sidney spoke but little,
and replied only in monosyllables to her, yet she
could see the change was telling upon him, and
she felt that there would come a time when he
would be his dear old self again. When the day
was over, her own troubles began. In her own
room, she thought of the father whom she had

abandoned—of *his* loneliness, left behind at his
work in that front top room, which had been home
to her.   She was not sorry that she had left him,
for there was an old promise, an old love for Sidney, to buoy her up; but she was very, very sorry
that they had parted in anger, and that her father
had resented a step in which his Christian charity
should have at once encouraged her.   By and bye it
would all come right; her father would understand
her and her motives; by and bye, when Sidney had
become reconciled to his lot in life, and there were
no more duties to fulfil, she would return home,
unasked even, and offer to be again the daughter
whom her father had professed to love.   For the
present, life in Sidney's home, doing her duty by
him whom she loved best in the world; she could
not let him suffer, and not do her best to work a
change in him.

Mattie worked a change—a great one.   The
instinct that assured her she possessed that power
had not deceived her; and Sidney, though he became never again his former self, altered for the
better.   This change strengthened Mattie in her

resolves, and made amends for her father's silence. She had written to Mr. Gray a long letter a few days after she had left his home, explaining her conduct more fully, entering more completely into the details of her former relations to the Hinchfords and the friends she had found in them; trusting that her father would believe that she loved him none the less for the step which she had taken—she who would have been more happy had he consented thereto—and hoping for the better days when she could return and take once more her place beside him. She had also asked in her letter that her box might be sent her, and he had considered that request as the one object of her writing, and responded to it by the transmission of the box and its contents, keeping back all evidence of his own trouble and anger. She had chosen her lot in life, he thought; she had preferred a stranger's home to her own flesh and blood; in the face of the world's opinion she had gone to nurse a man of three and twenty years of age. After all, she had never loved her father; he had come too late in life before her, and it was his fate never to gain

affection from those on whose kind feelings he had
a claim. He had been unlucky in his loves, and
he must think no more of them. His troubles
were earthly, and on earthly affections he must not
dwell too much--he must teach himself to soar
above them all.

He read the Bible more frequently than ever,
attended less to his work, and more to his district
society and local preaching; by all the means in
his power he turned his thoughts away from Mattie.
When the thought was too strong for him, he connected her with the wrong that she had done him,
and so thought uncharitably of her, as good men
have done before and since his time—good people
being fallible and liable to err.

Mattie knew nothing of her father's trouble, and
judged him as she had seen him last—angry
and uncharitable and jealous! That is a bad habit
of connecting friends whom we have given up
with the stormy scene which cut the friendship
adrift; of stereotyping the last impression—
generally the false one—and connecting *that*
with him and her for ever afterwards. Think

of the virtues that first drew us towards them, and not of the angry frown and the bitter word that set us apart; in the long run we shall find it answer, and have less wherewith to accuse ourselves.

Sidney Hinchford, whom we are forgetting, altered then for the better slowly but surely—even imperceptibly to himself. Still, when Mattie had been a month with him, and he looked back upon the feelings which had beset him before she took her place in his home, the change struck him at last. He could appreciate the kindness and self-denial that had brought her there, gladdened his home, and made his heart lighter. He could take pleasure in speaking with her of the old times, of his father, of his early days in Suffolk Street—in hearing her read to him, in being led into an argument with her, which promoted a healthy excitation of the mind, in walking with her when the days were fine. He was grateful for her services, and touched by them—she was his sister, whom he loved very dearly, and whom to part with would be another trial in store for him some day—and he had thought his trials were at an end long since!

Sidney Hinchford, be it observed here, made but a clumsy blind man; he had little of that con-centrativeness of the remaining senses, which make amends for the deprivation of one faculty. He neither heard better, nor was more sensitive to touch—and of this he complained a little peevishly, as though he had been unfairly dealt with.

"I haven't even been served like other blind folk," he said; "your voice startles me at times as though it were strange to me."

On one topic he would never dwell upon—the Wesdens. Mattie, true to the dying wish of the old man, attempted to bring the subject round to Harriet—Harriet, who was true to him yet, she be-lieved—but the subject vexed him, and evinced at once all that new irritability which had been born with his affliction.

"Let the past die—it is a bitter memory, and I dislike it," he would say; "now let us talk of the business which you think of setting me up in, and seeing me off in, before all the money is spent on housekeeping."

Mattie turned to that subject at his request—it

was one that pleased and diverted him. He was glad to speak of business; it sounded as if he were not quite dead yet. Mattie and he had spent many an hour in dilating upon the chances of opening a shop with the residue of the money which Sidney had saved before his illness—what shop it should be, and how it should be attended! He had only one reason for delaying the prosecution of the scheme—Mattie had implied more than once that when a shopkeeper was found, she should give up constant attendance upon him, and only call now and then to make sure that he was well, and not being imposed upon.

"To think of turning shopkeeper in my old age!" he said one day, with quite a cheerful laugh at his downfall; "I, Sidney Hinchford, bank clerk, who had hoped to make a great name in the city. Well, it is commerce still, and I shall have a fair claim to respectability, as the wholesalers say, if I don't give short weight, or false measure, Mattie."

"To be sure you will. But why do you not settle your mind to one business? Every day, Mr. Sidney, you think of a new one!"

"You must not blame me for that, Mattie," he replied; "I want to make sure of the most suitable, to find one in which I could take part myself."

"What do you think of the old business in which Mr. Wesden made money?—think of that whilst I am gone."

"Where are you going now?" he asked a little irritably.

"To scold the butcher for yesterday's tough joint," said Mattie.

"Butchers make money, but how the deuce could I chop up a sheep without personal damage?" he said, rambling off to a new idea.

Mattie hurried to the door. The butcher was certainly there; but, crossing the road in the direction of the house, Mattie had seen Harriet Wesden. The butcher was dismissed, and Harriet admitted silently into the passage.

"How long have *you* been here?" Harriet exclaimed.

"A month now. I promised his father that I would do my best for *him* left behind in trouble. You—you don't blame me?"

" Blame you!—no. Why should I?"

" My father thought that I was wrong to come here—exceeding my duty to my neighbour, and outraging my duty towards him. But I am not sorry."

" And Sid—how is he now? Why does he bear so much malice in his heart against me, as to refuse me admittance to his house?" she asked.

" He bears no malice, Harriet; but the past is painful to him. Presently he will come round, and judge all things truly. Every day he is less morbid—more resigned."

" I am glad of that."

" After all, everything has turned out for the best, Harriet," said Mattie.

" Prove that," was her quick answer.

Mattie was attempting the difficult task of deciphering the real thoughts of Harriet Wesden ;— what she regretted, and what she rejoiced at, now the picture was finished, and all its deep shadowing elaborated.

" For the best that the engagement was ended, Harriet. Think of the affliction that has befallen

him, and which would have parted him and you at
last."

"Why parted us?—do you think, had it befallen
me, that he would have turned away with horror—
that he would not have loved me all the better, and
striven all the harder to render my trouble less
heavy to be borne? Mattie, I knew that this
would come upon him years ago, and I did not
shrink from my engagement."

"You could never have married him—he is a
poor man, and may be poorer yet; it is impossible
to say."

"It is all over now, and this is idle talk, Mattie.
I have given up all thought of him, as he has
given up all thought of me —and perhaps it *is* for
the best," she added.

"We will hope so, Harriet."

"I was always a foolish and vain girl, prone to
change my mind, and scarcely knowing what that
mind was," she said bitterly. "It is easy enough
to forget."

Mattie scarcely understood her. She shook her
head in dissent, and would have turned the con-

versation by asking after her father's health—
Harriet's own health, which was not very evident on
her pale cheeks just then. Harriet darted away
from the subject.

" Well—all well," she said; " and how is Sidney
in health, you have not told me that ?"

" Better in health. I have said that his mind
is more at ease."

" Mattie, though I have given him up for ever,
though I know that I am nothing to him now, and
deserve to be nothing, let me see him again ! I am
going into the country with father for a week or
two, and should like to see him once more before
I go."

" Harriet, you love him still ! You are not glad
that it is all ended between you !"

" I should have been here in your place—I have
a right to be here !" she said, evasively.

" Tell him so."

Mattie had turned pale, but she pointed to the
parlour with an imperious hand. Harriet shrank
from the boldness of the step, and turned pale also.

" I—I— "

"This is no time for false delicacy between you and him," said Mattie; "he loves you in his heart —he is only saddened by the past belief that you loved Maurice Darcy—if you do not shrink to unite your fate with his, and make his life new and bright again, ask him to be your husband. In his night of life he dare not ask you now."

"I cannot do that," murmured Harriet; "that is beyond my strength."

"You and your father with him in his affliction, taking care of him and rendering him happy! All in your hands, and you shrink back from him!"

"Not from him, but from the bitterness of his reply to me," said Harriet. "Would you dare so much in my place?"

"I—I think so . But then," she added, "I do not understand what true love is—you said so once, if you remember."

Harriet detected something strange and new in Mattie's reply; she looked at Mattie, who was flushed and agitated. For the first time in her life, a vague far-off suspicion seemed to be approaching her.

"I will go in and see him—I will be ruled by what he says to me. Leave me with him, Mattie."

With her own impulsiveness, which had led her right and wrong, she turned the handle of the parlour door, and entered the room, where the old lover, blind and helpless, sat.

CHAPTER III.

THE OLD LOVERS.

YES, there he was, the old lover! The man whom she had once believed she should marry and make happy—whom she had valued at his just worth when he cast her off as unworthy of the love he had borne her. She had not seen him since that time ; he had held himself aloof from her, although he had talked of remaining still her friend, and the change in him was pitiable to witness.

It was the same handsome face, for all its pallor, and deep intensity of thought; the same intellectuality expressed therein, for all the blindness which had come there, and given that strange unearthly look to eyes still clear and bright, and which turned towards her, and startled her with their expression yet. But he was thin and wasted, and his hand, which rested on the table by his side, was an old man's hand, seared by age, and trembling as with palsy.

"What a time you have been, Mattie! Ah! you are growing tired of me at last," he said, with the querulousness characteristic of illness, but before then ever so uncharacteristic of him.

"Miss—Miss Wesden called to ask how you were," said Harriet, in a low voice.

"Indeed!" he said, after a moment's deliberation of that piece of information; "and you answered her, and let her go away, sparing me the pain of replying for myself. That's well and kind of you, Mattie. We are better by ourselves now."

"Yes."

Harriet dropped into a chair by the door, and clasped her hands together; he spoke firmly; he spoke the truth as he thought, and she accepted it for truth, and said no more.

Sidney Hinchford, oblivious of the visitor facing him, and composed in his blindness, detected no difference in the voice. Mattie's voice, we have remarked at an earlier stage of this narrative, closely

resembled Harriet's, and acuteness of ear had not
been acquired yet by the old lover.

"Mattie, I have been thinking of a new business
for us, since you have been gone."

"For us?" gasped Harriet.

"Ah! for us, if I can persuade you to remain
my housekeeper, and induce your father to extend
his consent. I have no other friend—I look to
you, girl—you must not desert me yet!"

"No."

"I fancy the stationery business, with you to
help me, Mattie, would be best, after all. You are
used to it, and I could sit in the parlour and take
stock, and help you with the figures in the accounts. I was always clever at mental arithmetic,
and it don't strike me that I shall be quite a dummy.
And then when I am used to the place—when I
can find the drawers, and know what is in them, I
shall be an able custodian of the new home, capa-
ble of minding shop while you go to your friends
for awhile. Upon my honour, Mattie, I'm quite
high-spirited about this—say it's a bargain, girl?"

Harriet answered in the affirmative for Mattie.

She had assumed her character and could not escape. She had resolved to go away, and make no sign to him of her propinquity; he cared not for her now; he dismissed her with a passing nod; it was all Mattie—Mattie in whom he believed and trusted, and on whose support in the future he built upon from that day! She knew how the story would end for him and Mattie—a peaceful and happy ending, and what both had already thought of, perhaps—let it be so, she was powerless to act, and it was not her place to interfere. Mattie had deceived her; it was natural—but she saw no longer darkly through the glass; beyond there was the successful rival, whom Sidney Hinchford would marry out of gratitude!

Sidney continued to dilate upon the prospects in life before him. Harriet had risen, and was standing with her hand upon the door, watching her opportunity to escape.

"Who would have dreamed of a man becoming resigned to an utter darkness, Mattie? Who would have thought of me in particular, cut out for a man of action, with no great love for books, or for anything that fastened me down to the domesticities ?"

" You are resigned, then ?"

" Well—almost."

" I am very glad."

" Why are you standing by the door, Mattie ? Why don't you sit down and talk a little of this business of ours ?"

" Presently."

" Now—just for a little while.   Leave Ann Packet to the lower regions—I'm as talkative to-day as an old woman of sixty.   Why, you will not balk me, Mattie ?"

" No."

" Read this for me—I have been trying if I can write in the dark—my first attempt at a benighted penmanship."

He held a paper towards her, and Harriet left her post by the door to receive it from his hands.

The writing was large and irregular, but distinct. She shivered as she read the words. The story she had seen so plainly, was more evident than ever.

" *Sidney Hinchford,*" she read, "*saved from shipwreck by Mattie Gray !*"

" And Mattie Gray here at my side accounts for my resignation," said he, laying his hand upon Harriet's. "Mattie, the old friend—after all, the best and truest !"

Harriet did not reply; she shrank more and more, cowering from him as though he saw her there, the unwelcome guest who had forced herself upon him.

" You are going out," he said, noticing the glove upon the hand he had relinquished now.

" Yes, for a little while."

" Don't be long. Where are you going that I cannot accompany you ?"

" On business—I shall be back in an instant."

" Very well," he said, with a half-sigh ; "but remember that you have chosen yourself to be my protector, sister, friend, and that I cannot bear you too long away from me. I wish I were more worthy of your notice—that I could return it in some way or fashion not distasteful to you. Sometimes I wish——"

" Say no more!" cried Harriet, with a vehemence that startled him ; " I am going away."

The door clanged to and left him alone. She had .hurried from the room, shocked at the folly, the mockery of affection which had risen to his lips. Ah! he was a fool still, he thought ; he had frightened Mattie by hovering on the verge of that proposal, which he had considered himself bound to make perhaps, out of gratitude for the life of servitude Mattie had chosen for herself. He had been wrong ; he had taken a mean advantage, and rendered Mattie's presence there embarrassing ; his desire to be grateful had scared her from him, as well it might—he, a blind man, prating of affection! He had been a fool and coward ; he would seal his lips from that day forth, and be all that was wished of him—nothing more. Harriet had made her escape into the narrow passage, had contrived to open the street-door, and was preparing to hurry away, when Mattie came towards her.

" Going away without a good-bye, Harriet!"

" I had forgotten," she said coldly.

"What have you said to him?—have you—have you——"

"I have said nothing at which yon have reason to feel alarmed," said Harriet; "I have not taken your advice. He thinks and speaks only of you, and I did not break upon his thoughts by any harsh reminiscences."

"You are excited, Harriet; don't go away yet, with that look. What does it mean?"

"Nothing."

"Has he offended you?"

"No."

"Have I?"

"No," was the cold reiteration. "I am not well. I ought not to have intruded here. I see my mistake, and will not come again."

"I hope you will, many, many times. I build upon you assisting me in the good work I have begun here. You and I together, in the future, striving for the old friend, Sidney Hinchford."

"I am going away to-morrow—it is doubtful when I shall return, or what use I shall be to either you or him.   You understand him better than I."

"I do not understand you this afternoon," said
Mattie, surveying her more intently; "what have
I done?   Don't you," she added, as a new thought
of hers seemed to give a clue to Harriet's, " think
it right that I should be here!"

"If you think so, Mattie, it cannot matter what
my opinion is."

"Yes—to me."

"You came hither with the hope of befriend-
ing him, as a sister might come? On your honour,
with no other motive ?"

"On my honour, with none other."

"Why deceive him, then?" was the quick rejoinder; "why tell him that your father gave his
consent for your stay here, when he was so opposed
to it?"

"He thought so from the first, and I did not
undeceive him, lest he should send me away. Have
you seen my father ?"

"He called last night at our house.   He is
anxious and distressed about you."

"I am sorry."

" He thinks that you have no right to be here—
I think you have now."

" Oh ! Harriet, you do not think——"

" Hush! say nothing. You are your own mistress, and I am not angry with you. You have
been too good a friend of mine, for me to envy any
act of kindness towards him I loved once. I don't
love him now."

" You said you did."

" A romantic fancy—I have been romantic from
a child. It is all passed away now—remember that
when he——"

" When he—*what?*"

" Asks you to be his wife, to become his natural
protector ; you alone can save him now from deso-
lation—never my task—never now my wish. Good-
bye."

She swept away coldly and proudly, leaving the
amazed Mattie watching her departure. What
did she mean ?—what had Sidney said to her that
she should go away like that, distrusting her and
the motives which had brought her there—she, of
all women in the world!

Mattie went back to Sidney's room excited and trembling. Close to his side before she startled him by her voice.

"Mr. Sidney, long ago you were proud of being straightforward in your speech—of telling the plain truth, without prevarication."

"Time has not changed me, I hope, Mattie."

" What have you said to Harriet Wesden?"

" To whom!"

The horror on his face expressed the facts of the case at once, before the next words escaped him.

" It was—Harriet Wesden then!"

" Yes."

" And she came in to see me, and assumed your character, Mattie?" he said; " why did you let her in?"

" I don't know," murmured Mattie ; " she was anxious about you, and she had come hither to make inquiries without intruding upon you, until I—I advised her to come."

" For what reason?" he asked in a low tone.

"I thought that you two might become better friends again, and——"

"Ah! no more of that," he interrupted; "that was like my good sister Mattie, striving for everybody's happiness, except her own, perhaps. Mattie, you talk as if I had my sight, and were strong enough to win my way in life yet. You so quick of perception, and with such a knowledge of the world—you!" he reiterated.

"Misfortune will never turn Harriet Wesden away from any one whom she has loved—it would not stand in the way of any true woman. And oh! sir, if I may speak of her once again—just this once—"

"You may not," was his fierce outcry; "Mattie, I ask you not, in mercy to me!"

"Why?" persisted Mattie.

"I don't know—let me be in peace."

It was his old sullenness—his old gloom. Back from the past, into which Mattie's efforts had driven it, stole forth that morbid despondency which had kept him weak and hopeless. The re-

mainder of that day the old enemy was too strong
for any effort of Sidney's strange companion, and
Mattie felt disheartened by her ill success.

CHAPTER IV.

A NEW DECISION.

SIDNEY HINCHFORD rose the next morning in better spirits, and Mattie in worse. Half the night in his own room Sidney had reflected on his vexatious sullenness of the preceding day, and on the effect it must have had on Mattie; half the night, Mattie in her room had pondered on the strangeness of the incidents of the last four-and-twenty hours—on that new demeanour of Harriet Wesden, which implied so much, and yet explained so little.

After all, Mattie thought, was she right in staying there? Had she treated her father well in leaving him without a fair confession of that truth which she had breathed into the ears of a dying man, and scarcely owned till then unto herself.

She had not come there with any sinister design of winning, by force as it were, a place in Sidney Hinchford's heart; she had never dreamed for an instant—she did not dream then!—of ever be-·coming his wife, with a right to take her place at his side and fight his battles for him.

She had been actuated by motives the purest and the best—but who believed her? Had not her father mistrusted her? Had not Harriet, who understood her so well she thought, regarded her as one scheming for herself?—she whose only scheme was to bring two lovers together once more, and see them happy at each other's side. For an instant she had not thought that she was "good enough" for Sidney Hinchford; she who had been an outcast from society, an object of suspicion to the police, a beggar, and a thief! No matter that she had been saved from destruction and was now living an exemplary life, or that misfortune had altered Sidney and rendered him dependent on another's help, he was still the being above her by birth, education, position, and she could but offer him disgrace.

With that conviction impressed upon her, conscious that Sidney had improved and would continue to improve, an object of distrust to her best friends—why not to the neighbours who watched them about the streets and talked about them? —only judged fairly and honourably by him she served, was it right to stop—was there any need for further stay there?

She was thinking of this over breakfast—afterwards in her little business round, during which period another visitor had forced himself into Sidney's presence, without exercising much courtesy in the effort. Ann Packet had opened the street door, and looked inclined to shut it again, had not the visitor forestalled her—she was never very quick in her movements—by springing on to the mat, and thence with a bound to the parlour door.

"Oh, my goodness! you mustn't go in there. Master left word that you were never to be shown into him again on any pertence."

"Where's Mattie?"

"Gone out for orders," said Ann. "Just step in this room, sir, and wait a bit."

"Young woman, I shall do nothing of the kind. When my daughter comes in, tell her where I am. That's your business; mind it, if you please."

Mr. Gray turned the handle of the door, and walked into the room.

"Good morning, Mr. Hinchford."

Sidney recognized that voice at least—the voice of a man who had worried him to death with his religious opinions—and his face lengthened.

"You here?"

"Yes, I have come again," he answered, drawing a chair close to the table, and confronting Sidney. "I suppose you thought that I had given you up as irreclaimable."

"I had hoped so," was the dry answer.

"Given my daughter up, too."

"No; that wasn't likely."

"Indeed—why not?"

"We don't give up our best friends, those who have won upon our hearts most, in a hurry."

"Do you mean that for me, or is that another side to your confounded obstinacy? Won't you give her up to me, her father?"

"If you wish it. I cannot set myself in opposition to you. The remembrance of a dear father of my own would not lead me, did I possess the power, to stand in opposition to you."

"You—will side with me, then, in telling her that it is not right to stay here?"

"Not right! You thought so once?"

"Not for an instant."

"She is here with your consent?"

"Did she tell you that? Don't please say that my Mattie ever told you that?"

Sidney considered. No, she had not said so, he remembered.

"She came against my will, full of a foolish idea of doing you good, and no power of mine could stop her," said Gray.

"Against your will?"

"I said she did," said Mr. Gray, sharply; "don't you believe me?"

"Yes—I believe you. But this is very singular."

Sidney bit his nails, and reflected on this new discovery, After a few moments he said,

"Mr. Gray, I have been forgiving you all the past torture for the sake of your kindness in allowing Mattie to constitute herself my guardian."

"Rubbish !"

"My guardian angel, I might say; for she has saved me from despair, and turned my thoughts away from many deep and bitter things. I was turning against myself, my life, my God, in the very despair of being of use in the world, and she saved me. Do you blame her coming now?"

Mr. Gray took time to consider that question. He bit his nails in his turn, and looked steadily at the young man, who had altered very much for the better.

" I don't find fault with the result—there !" and Mr. Gray looked as though he had made a great concession.

" You would not be a true minister if you did," said Sidney; " and you are not a true father if you don't value the sterling gold in Mattie's character. Pure gold, with no dross in the crucible—not an atom's worth, as I'm a living sinner !"

" We're all living sinners, young man," said he,

getting up and beginning to pace the room, as he
had paced it, preaching meanwhile, a month ago,
and nearly driven Sidney Hinchford out of his
mind.

"Do you object to sitting down?" asked Sidney,
after bearing with these heavy perambulations for
a time.

"Presently; I am going to speak to you in a
minute."

"Not in the old fashion, please," said Sidney,
quite plaintively; "although I can put up with more
now ; for Mattie's sake I'll even listen to a sermon,
if you'll give me fair warning when you're going
to begin, and how long it is likely to last."

"For your soul's sake, as well as Mattie's, you
mean, I hope?"

"Anything—anything you like!"

"As careless of heavenly matters as ever, I
believe.   The task of reformation still unperformed
—perhaps left for me, unworthy instrument that
I am."

"Exactly."

"Eh?"

"We are all unworthy instruments as well as living sinners, you know," said Sidney, drily.

"And flippant, too—and on such a subject! But we shall change you in good time."

"And this morning, now, you will let me off with a small sermon?"

"I haven't come to sermonize to-day," replied Mr. Gray, severely, "therefore do not give way to any groundless fears of torturing on my part."

"Thank you—thank you!"

"I have come to test your sense of justice—fairness of what is due to me from you, and Mattie."

"Test it, friend."

"Give me back my daughter!"

"Why, that's what Brabantio says in the play; but I'll give you a more gracious answer than he got. If you wish her to return with you—why, she must. I would not stop her," he added, with a sigh, "if it were in my power."

"You will persuade her to return with me."

"Was she happy with you?"

"Until your father died—yes."

"I will tell her," said Sidney; "that there is right on your side—Mattie will see that. There was right on hers, too, for she had made a solemn promise to a dying man, and she knew well enough that I was desolate. I will persuade her even, if you wish it, but——"

"Go on."

"But what harm is she doing here?"

"What harm!" echoed Mr. Gray, with an elevated voice; "why, harm to that good name which she has kept for years. What do you fancy people think of her being in this house?—her a stranger to you by blood, and you so young! Sir, she has risked her character by staying here—and I very much doubt if the world is likely to believe her own version of this extraordinary freak."

"Do you believe it?" asked Sidney.

"Well—I do."

"And I also—that makes two out a very few for whose good opinion Mattie Gray cares."

"Whilst we are in the world we should care for the world's opinion, Mr. Hinchford."

"I think not, when it's a false one. You, a minister, telling me to study the world!"

"I never said that—how aggravating you are, to be sure!"

"Pardon me," said Sidney, quickly; "a misinterpretation, Mr. Gray. And we must study the world after all—you're right enough. Poor Mattie, what would she think of this hiss of slander in her ears?"

"I warned her of it—and she braved me."

"Ah! a brave girl, whose reward will come in a brighter world than this. Well," he added, sadly, "go she must. I agree with you."

"I am very much obliged to you—I am going to shake hands with you."

Mr. Gray and Sidney Hinchford shook hands. Sidney held the minister's tightly in his grip whilst he uttered the next words.

"You will bring her with you now and then, to hinder me from wholly sinking back," he said; "remember that she is but the one old friend of the past whom I care to know is by my side, and in whom I can trust. Remember what she found me, what she leaves me, and if you are not wholly selfish, you will not always keep her away."

Mr. Gray was touched by this appeal—his old jealousy vanished completely—he was proud in his heart of this young man's interest in Mattie.

"I promise that—until we go away, that is, of course."

"Go away!—whither?"

"Oh! nothing is settled—there was a little talk of appointing me a missionary abroad some time ago—a preacher at a foreign station, where the benighted require stirring words, and the preacher is expected to be continually stirring—preaching, I mean. But it is only talk, perhaps—they may have found a better man," he added, a little tetchily.

"Should you care to leave England?"

"Care, sir!—it is my great ambition to do good—to make amends for the evil of my early life."

"Ah!—yes."

Sidney had become absent in his manner—Mr. Gray, who had become voluble, discoursed at great length on his peculiar principle of doing good, but

Sidney heard but little of his argument, and was engrossed by thoughts of the change coming unto him again, and to which he could not offer opposition.   Discoursing thus, and thinking thus, when Mattie returned, and stood in the doorway, looking from father to friend.

"Father," she ejaculated at last.

"Don't say that you are sorry to see me, after this long parting !" he exclaimed, as he rose in an excited manner, and went towards her with both hands outstretched.

"Not sorry—no—but very, very glad !"

She held his hands, and leaned forward to kiss him.   He caught her to his heart then, and the tears welled into his eyes at this evidence of the past parting having been forgotten and forgiven.

"Mattie," he said, " I have been thinking of all this again—over and over again, patiently, and not in anger—and I still think that it is wrong to stay here."

" And he—what does he think ?" looking towards Sidney.

Sidney answered for himself.

"That, perhaps, we are both too young—blind though I am, and pure as you are, Mattie—to keep house together after this fashion. For your sake, I will ask you to go back with your father. I have been wrong and selfish."

"I said that I would go when you wished it, Mr. Sidney."

"I wish it, then!"

"Very well."

"Go—to return again very frequently with your father, and see that I am well, and likely to do well. Mattie, for ever after this understand that I cannot do utterly without you. Wrong and selfish also in that wish, perhaps, but I am sure of you forgiving me!"

"Yes—yes," she said, hurriedly. "It is strange that we three should all have been thinking of going away to-day—and perhaps," with a blush, "it was scarcely right to come. But," evincing here her old rebellious spirit, with a suddenness that made her father and Sidney leap again, "if he were the same man I found here first, I would have stopped—mark that!"

"Yes, but he isn't, my dear!" said Mr. Gray,
cowed into submission, and afraid of Mattie talking
herself into a change of mind; "so it's all happened for the best, and we are all thankful, and—
all friends!"

"I will be ready when you wish, then."

"I have ordered a cab to come round at twelve.
You see I was sure that you would not turn against
me ever again."

"I never turned against you—don't think that."

Mattie went out of the room—was a long while
gone—returned with her eyes red and swollen, as
though she had been weeping. The cab at the
same time rattled up to the door, and Ann Packet
—with red and swollen eyes also, if she could have
been seen just then—was heard struggling down-
stairs with Mattie's box, which she had not allowed
Mattie to touch.

"Go and talk to Mr. Sidney again, gal. You
mayn't have another chance," she had said, and
Mattie had started and glared at her as at a phantom. Surely it was time for her to go, when this
faithful but dull-witted woman saw through the

veil which she believed had hidden her true heart from every one on earth. But that must be fancy, she thought, and she went back to the room to bid Sidney good-bye, and to check the thanks with which he would have overwhelmed her.

"No thanks, sir—only my duty to one whose last thoughts were of your happiness, and how it was best to promote it. *He* had faith in me, and I have endeavoured to deserve it, as though he had been watching every action of my own from heaven. Good-bye, Mr. Sidney."

"Good-bye—best of friends. You will not desert me wholly?--your father is on my side now."

"Yes. I shall look in upon you very often, I hope—and you must keep strong, and make up your mind about that business—and—and not think yourself into that low estate ever again. Now I am ready to go."

Mattie and her father left the house the former had brightened by her presence. In the cab she struggled for awhile with her forced composure, and then burst forth into irrepressible tears.

"Patience, Mattie.   I see the end to this.   All's well."

"You see the end to this ?   No, you cannot !"

" Oh ! yes—I can."

Mr. Gray uttered not a syllable more during the remainder of the journey ; and Mattie, ashamed of her tears, dried her eyes, and asked no further questions.

CHAPTER V.

ANN PACKET EXPRESSES AN OPINION.

SIDNEY HINCHFORD knew that he should miss
Mattie, and accordingly made up his mind, as he
thought, to the loss. But there is no making up
one's mind entirely to the absence of those we love,
and upon whom we have been dependent, and
Sidney found himself no exception to the rule.

In great things he had expected to miss her, but
in the thousand minor ones, wherein she had
reigned dominant without his knowledge, he made
no calculation for, and a hundred times a day they
suggested the absence of the ruling genius. The
house assumed an unnatural and depressing still-
ness ; he felt wholly shut from the world again—
no one to whom he could speak, or who, in reply,
could assure him that his lot was not worse than

other people's, and that there lay before him many methods for its amelioration.

He became more dull and thoughtful ; but he did not sink back to his past estate—that was a promise which he had made Mattie, before she went away. When she came again—he prayed it might be soon—she should not find him the despondent, morbid being, from which her efforts had transformed him. He tried to think the time away by dwelling upon that business in which he intended to embark ; but there came the grave perplexity of the general management—and whom to trust, now Mattie had returned to her father's home ! Meanwhile, he was wasting money by inaction, and he had always known the value of money, and money's fugitive properties, if not carefully studied.

We say that he tried to think of his new business life, for other thoughts would force their way to the front, and take pre-eminence. He could not keep the past ever in the background ; before him would flit, despite his efforts to escape it, the figure of his lost love, to whom he had looked forward once as his solace in his blindness. Blindness, with her at his side, had not appeared a life to be deplored, and it was ever pleasant to picture what might have been, had the ties between them never been sundered by his will. For he loved her still—the stern interdict upon her name was even a part of his affection; and there were times when he did not care to shut her from his mind—on the contrary, loved to think of her as he had known her once. In these latter days, he thought of both Harriet and Mattie—drew, as was natural to one in his condition, the comparison between them—saw which was the truer, firmer, better character, but loved the weaker for all that! That Harriet had not loved him truly and firmly, did not matter; he had given her up for his pride's sake, even for her own sake, but he loved her none the less. She would have been unhappy with him after a while—she could not have endured the place of nurse and comforter—she, who was made for the brightness of life, and to be comforted herself when that brightness was shut from her; she was not like Mattie, a woman of rare character and energy.

Mattie troubled him. She had awakened his
gratitude ; the last day her father had aroused in
him his fears that she had rendered herself open to
the suspicions of the world by her efforts in his service
—he had not thought of *that* before ! Mattie's character was worth studying—it was so far apart from
the common run of womankind—she had treasured
every past action that stood as evidence of kindness to her, and made return for it a thousandfold.
Who would have dreamed of all this years ago, when
he tracked her with the police to the Kent Street
lodging-house, and was moved to pity by her
earnest eyes ? Hers had been a strange life ; his
had been exceptional—his had ended in blank
monotony, that nothing could change—what was in
store for her ? He thought of the mistake that he
had committed on the day that Harriet had per-
sonated her unwillingly, and blushed for the error
of the act. He had been moved too much by gratitude, and had almost offered his blank life to
Mattie, as he thought ; Mattie who would have
shrunk from him like the rest, had she believed
that he had had such thoughts of *her.* His blind-

ness had affected his mind; he had grown heedless,
foolish, wilful. Then his thoughts revolved
to Harriet Wesden again—to the girl who had not
lost her interest in him with her love, but had stolen
to his solitary house, to ask about him, and to note
the change in him. She had been always a
generous-hearted girl—moved at any trouble, and
anxious to take her part in its alleviation—there was
nothing remarkable in it. He was still the old
friend and playfellow, after all, and in the future
days, when their engagement lay further back from
the present, he should be glad to hear her voice of
sympathy again.

These thoughts, or thoughts akin to these, tra-
velled in a circle round the blind man's brain, hour
after hour, day after day. Thoughts of business,
Mattie, Harriet Wesden—varied occasionally by
the reminiscences of the dead father, and the relations who had sought him out, whom he had sought,
and then turned away from.

Mattie and her father came to see him three days
after their formal withdrawal from his home; that
was a fair evening, which changed the aspect of

things, and which he remembered kindly afterwards, notwithstanding a prayer of some duration,
that Mr. Gray contrived to introduce. Something
new to think of was always Sidney Hinchford's
craving, and the day that followed any fresh incidents bore less heavily upon him, as he rehearsed
those incidents in his mind.

Still they had said nothing of the business;
they had been more anxious to know how he had
spent his time since their departure, and whether
Mattie's absence had made much difference to him.
Sidney spoke the truth, and Mattie was pleased
at the confession. It was an evidence of
the good she had done by resisting her father's
will, and she was woman enough not to be sorry
for the result.

That evening, Ann Packet, bringing in the
supper to her master, was startled by the question
which he put to her.

" How is Mattie looking, Ann?"

" Looking, sir!"

" Has all this watching, studying my eccentri-
cities, affected her? "

"She's a little pale mayhap—but she has allus been pale since her last illness."

"I never gave a thought as to the effect which the constant study of a monomaniac might produce upon her," he said half abruptly; "but she's quit of me now, and will improve."

"Oh! she was well enough here—like a bird chirping about the house—Mattie likes something to do for some one. An extrornary girl, Master Sidney, as was ever sent to be a blessing unto all she took to."

"Yes—an extraordinary girl. Sit down."

"No—it isn't for the likes of me to do that here, sir."

"Sit down, and tell me what you think of her. We don't study appearances in trouble—and a blind man loves the sound of a woman's voice."

"Then you have altered werry much, sir."

"Yes—thanks to Mattie again."

"And to think that she was a little ragged gal about the streets, sir. Many and many a time have I crept to the door after shop was shut, and given her the odd pieces I could find, and she was allus grateful for 'em."

"Always grateful—who can doubt that?"

"She was waiting for the pieces when you came home and lost that brooch—poor ignorant thing, then, sir!"

"Through you then, Ann, we first knew Mattie Gray. Strangely things come round!"

"Ah! you don't know half her goodness, sir— she's just as kind to anybody who wants kind-ness—*just*."

"Yes, it is like her !"

"It's a pity her father isn't less of a fidget—she ought to have had a better un than that, or have never lighted on him, I think."

"Is she not happy with him, then?"

"She may be, she mayn't—but he *is* a fidget, and Mattie ought to have some one to take care of her now, and make her happy—like."

"A husband, you mean?"

"Yes, I think so."

"Sit down, Ann. Perhaps you know of some one who is likely to take care of Mattie in the way you think?"

"I don't know."

"Some one who calls and sees her, and in whom she is interested?"

"Oh! no—no one calls to see *her*," said Ann, "her father's jealous of her liking anybody save himself. I saw that long ago."

"I should like to see—ah, ha! *to see!*" he cried —"Mattie happy. She deserves it."

"Those who think so little of theirselves seldom find happiness though—do they, sir?"

Sidney started at the axiom—it was deeper than Ann Packet's general run of observations.

"There are so few of those good folk in the world, Ann."

"Mattie's one."

"Yes—Mattie's one!" he repeated.

"I've often wondered and a-wondered what would make her happy; do you know, sir, sometimes I think that—that *you* might, if you'll excuse an ignorant woman saying so."

"That I might!—what has made you think that? Sit down—why *don't* you sit down!"

"Well, just to talk this over, and for my darling's sake, I will for once demean myself;" and

Ann Packet, red in the face with excitement,
seated herself on the verge of the horsehair
chair.

Ann Packet had broken through the ice at last;
it had been a trouble of long duration; she who
knew Mattie's secret, guessed where Mattie's
chance of happiness rested, she thought.   But it is
delicate work to strive for the happiness of other
people, and leads to woful failures, as a rule.

Ann Packet was nervous; the plunge had been
made, and the truth must escape—she dashed into
the subject, for "her gal's sake."

"Lookee here, sir—it's no good my keeping
back my 'pinion, that our Mattie is really fond of
you! When she was a girl in Suffolk Street, and
you a bit of a boy, she used to worry me about
you, and yet I never guessed it! When she
growed bigger and you growed bigger, she showed
her liking less, but it peeped out at times unbe-
known to herself, and yet I never guessed it! But
when she was ill in Tenchester Street, and I left
here to nus her, the truth came on me all of a
heap, and mazed me drefful!"

"What made you think of this—this nonsense, then?" he asked.

"She spoke about you in her fever, when her head was gone," said Ann; "of how your happiness hadn't come, and yet she'd worked so hard for it. And somehow I guessed it then—and when she came here, and was, for the fust time, happy in her way—I knowed it!"

"Folly! folly!" murmured Sidney.

"And they who says that she had no right to come here, don't know the rights of things—she liked you best of all, sir, and she comes here, duty bound, to do her best. If they says a word aginst her in MY hearing for her coming here, let 'em look out, that's all!"

Sidney sat, with his fingers interlaced, thoughtful and grave.

"You may go now, Ann—I'm sorry that you have put this into my head. It can't be true."

"True or not, just ask her some day when you feel that you can't do without her help, and see who's wrong of us two. And you'll have to ask her, mind that!"

Ann rose and bustled towards the door. At the door a new form of argument suggested itself, and she came back again.

"You're blind enough not to care for good looks so much now—if you can get a good heart think yourself lucky, sir. You've just the chance of making one woman happy in your life, and in finding your life very different to what it is now, with a blundering gal like me to worry you. She won't think any the wus of you for being blind and helpless—she's much too good for you!"

" Well, that's true enough, Ann."

" I dont say that I'm saying this for your sake, young man," said Ann Packet in quite a maternal manner, " for you're no great catch to anybody, and will be a sight of trouble. But I do think that Mattie took a fancy to you ever so long ago, and that it didn't die away like other people's because you came to grief. And if my opinion has discumfrumpled you more than I expected, why, you asked for it, and I haven't many words to pick and choose from, when I've made up my mind to speak. And I'm not sorry now that I've spoke it any-ways."

"I fear Mattie would not thank you, Ann."

"Mattie never knowed what was good for herself so well as for t'other people—I looks after her good like her mother—I don't know that any one else would. And though I'm your servant, I'm her friend—and so I asks you, if you've any intentions, to speak out like a gentleman!"

Still suffering from nervous excitement, Ann Packet closed the door, and ran down-stairs to indulge in an hysterical kind of croaking, with her head in the dresser-drawer. It had been a great effort, but Ann had succeeded in it. Her young master knew the whole truth now, and there was no excuse for him. He must give up Mattie or marry her, she thought—either way her girl would not be "worrited" out of her life any longer!

Meanwhile the young master left his supper untouched, and dwelt upon the revelation. Something new to think of!—something to stir afresh the sluggish current of his life.

Was it true?—was it likely?—was it to be

helped, if true or likely?   Could it be possible
that it lay in his power to promote the happiness
of any living being still?   Could he make happy,
above all, the girl whom he had known so long,
and who had served him so faithfully?   He did
not think of himself, or ask if it were possible to
love her; possibly for the first time in his life,
he was wholly unselfish, and thought only of a
return for all the sacrifices *she* had made.   He
could remember now that hers had been a life of
abnegation—that she had risked her good name
once for Harriet Wesden—once, and in the latter
days, for himself.   All this simply Mattie's gratitude for the kindness extended in the old days
—nothing more.   It was not likely that that ignorant woman below could know all that had been un-
fathomable to brighter, keener intellects.

But if true, what better act on his part than to
gladden her heart, and add to the content of his
own?   He began a new existence with his loss of
sight—the old world vanished away completely, and
left him but one friend from it—let him not lose

that one by his perversity or pride. Still, let him do nothing hastily and shame both him and her. He would-wait!

CHAPTER VI.

MR. GRAY'S SCHEME.

MR. GRAY and his daughter Mattie re-commenced housekeeping together on a different principle. Mattie's flitting had impressed Mr. Gray with the consciousness of his daughter possessing a will a trifle more inflexible than his own, and he respected her opinions in consequence. He treated her less like a child, and more like a woman whose remarks were worth listening to. In plain truth, he had become a little afraid of Mattie. He had learned to love her, and was afraid of losing her. Her stern determination to keep her promise—even part with him, rather than break it—had won his respect; for he was a firm man himself, and in his heart admired firmness in others.

Father and daughter settled down to home-

matters, and worked together in many things; if
the daughter had one secret from her father, it
was the woman's natural aversion to confess to an
attachment not likely to be returned, and was
scarcely a secret, considering that Mr. Gray had
more than an inkling of the truth.

The father did not care to solve the problem that
was so easy of solution; he objected to showing any
interest in such trivial mundane matters as love-
making. He had a soul himself above love-making;
which he considered vain, frivolous, and worldly,
leading the thoughts astray from things divine.
He saw Mattie's perplexity, and even hoped in
the good time to alter it, if separation did not have
its proper effect. "Presently—we shall see," was
Mr. Gray's motto; and though he had spoken hope-
fully to Mattie, as Mattie had fancied, yet when
they were at home again—two prosaic home figures
—he kept the subject in the background.

Still he was watchful, and when Mattie began to
alter, to become more grave and downcast, as though
his home was not exactly the place where she
experienced happiness—when she brightened up at

any suggestion to visit Sidney Hinchford, he thought less of his own comfort, and more of his daughter's, like a good father as he was, after all.

One afternoon, without apprising that daughter of his intentions, he walked over to Camberwell, to see Sidney Hinchford. That young gentleman had ventured forth into the street, and therefore Mr. Gray had leisure to put things in order during his absence; arrange the mantel-piece, and wheel the table into the exact centre of the room. Anything out of order always put him in an ill temper, and he wanted to discuss business matters in an equable way, and with as little to disturb him as possible. If anything besides business leaked forth in the course of conversation, he should not be sorry; but he would take no mean advantage of Sidney Hinchford's position. He had a scheme to propose, which might be accepted or declined— what that scheme might end in, he would not say just then. It might end in his daughter marrying Sidney, or it might only tend to that singular young man's comfort and peace of mind—at all events, harm could not evolve from it, and possibly some personal advantage to himself, though he considered that *that* need not be taken into account.

Sidney Hinchford returned, and his face lit up at the brisk "Good afternoon" of Mr. Gray. He turned a little aside from him, as if expecting a smaller, softer hand in his, a voice more musical, asking if he were well, and then his face lost a great deal of its brightness with his disappointment.

"Alone?" he said.

"This time, Mattie is very busy—has a large dress-making order to fulfil."

"She'll kill herself with that needlework," he remarked; "it is a miserable profession, at the best."

"You're quite right, Mr. Sidney. And talking about professions, have you thought of yours lately?"

"Oh! I have thought of a hundred things. I must invest my capital—such as it is—in something."

"Will you listen patiently to a little plan of mine? I am of the world, worldly to-day, God forgive me!" he ejaculated, piously.

" What plan is that? Let us sit down and talk it over."

The local preacher, lithographer, &c., sat down facing Sidney, on whose face was visible an expression of keen interest. In matters of religion, Mr. Gray was long and prosy; in matters of business, quick and terse, a man after Sidney's own heart. Two "straightforward" men like them got through a deal of business in a little time.

" How much money have you at command ?"

" A hundred pounds, perhaps."

" So have I."

" What's that to do with it ?"

" A great deal, if you like my scheme—nothing, if you don't."

" Go on."

" A hundred pounds might start a business, but it's a risk—two hundred is better. How does Gray and Hinchford sound, now ?"

" A partnership ?"

" Why not? You're not fit to manage a business by yourself—I'm inclined to think the two of us might make a success of it—the three of us, if

Mattie has to assist. I don't see why we should go
on like this any longer—you can't stand at this
rent—one house may as well hold all of. us—why
not?"

"You are very kind. I shall be a great trouble
to you."

"I hope not. If you are—I like trouble. I
shall make a bright light of you in good time!"

Sidney thought of the sermons in store for him,
but hazarded no comment. Beyond them, and before all, was the preacher's daughter—the woman
who understood him, and who had even rendered
blindness endurable.

"You were speaking a short while since of going
abroad. Have you changed your mind?"

"They changed theirs at the chapel. Bless you!
they thought they could pitch upon a man so much
more suitable! You hear that—so much more
suitable!"

"Ah!—a good joke."

"I don't see where the joke lies," he said quickly.

"I beg pardon. No, not exactly a joke—was
it?"

"I should say not."

"Well—and this business—what is it to be ?"

"I fancy the old idea of a bookseller and stationer's. I can bring a little connection from our chapel together—and there's your friends at the bank."

"No—don't build on them—I have done with them."

"Ah ! I had forgotten. But we must not bear enmity in our hearts against our fellow-men."

"True—and this business—where is it to be ?"

"We'll look out, Mattie and I, at once."

"Nothing settled yet, then ?" said Sidney, with a sigh, who was anxious to be stirring in life once more.

"Nothing yet, of course. I did not know whether you would approve of the scheme. Whether Mattie and I would be exactly fitting company for you."

"Is that satire ?"

"My dear sir, I never said a satirical thing in my life."

"The best of company, then—for you and Mattie

are the only friends left me, save that honest girl down-stairs."

" Ah ! Ann Packet—we must not forget her, or we shall have Mattie scolding us."

" I asked if it were satire, because you are doing me a great service, and saving me from much anxiety. I have been thinking lately that it would be better for me to find my way into some asylum or other, and settle down there apart from the busy world without. You come forward to save me from the streets I have been fearing."

" As Mattie was saved," said Mr. Gray, solemnly; " remember that!"

Mr. Gray shortly afterwards took his leave. The same night he communicated the details of his scheme to his daughter; he could easily read in her face that it was a plan that had her full concurrence. Sidney at home again—Sidney to take care of, and screen from all those ills to which his position was liable !

In a short while a shop in the suburbs of London—not a great distance from Peckham Rye —was found to let. It stood in a new neighbourhood, with houses rising round it at every turn. A building mania had set in that direction, and a populous district was springing up there.

"I have always heard that to pitch one's camp in a new neighbourhood, if one has the patience to wait, will always succeed. We three have patience, and I think we'll try it."

This was said to Mattie, after she and her father had inspected the premises, and were walking by cross roads towards Camberwell, to gladden Sidney with the latest news.

"We'll try it—we'll begin home there, father."

"Home in earnest—eh?"

Mattie did not notice the meaning in his tones; she was full of other thoughts.

"It must be a home, that you and I will try to render happy for him—for his own sake—for his dead father's," she said.

"To be sure. And if he be not happy then, it will not be our fault."

"I hope not!"

"Hope not," said her father; "do you think we may fail in the attempt?"

"If we be not careful. We must remember that he is weak and requires support—that he is blind, and cannot escape us if we weary him too much."

"Oh! I see—I see," he said, a little aggrieved; "you are afraid that I shall tire him with the Word of God. Mattie, he's not exactly a Christian man yet, and I should certainly like to make him one. There will be plenty of time for preaching the truth unto him."

"And for leaving it alone."

"Bless my soul!" he ejaculated, as though Mattie had fired a pistol in his ear.

"You will believe that I understand him best, and I think that it will not do to attack him too often with our creed. His first disappointment is over—he is teaching himself resignation—he will come round to a great extent without our help—with our help, judiciously applied, he will come round altogether."

"You think a man may be told too often of the error of his ways?"

"Yes."

"Then we shall never agree upon that point."

And they never did. Notwithstanding this, Mr. Gray remembered Mattie's hint, and often curbed a rising attempt to preach to Sidney. When his rigour carried him to preaching point, Sidney listened patiently; when Sidney knew that Mr. Gray's energy was real, and that not one atom of hypocrisy actuated his motives, he respected the preacher, and paid attention to him.

He altered rapidly for the better; he became again almost the Sidney Hinchford of old times— the smile returned more frequently, the brightness of his face was something new; it was pleasant to think that he was not isolated from the world, and that there were friends in it yet to care for him.

He went to church every Sunday in lieu of chapel, somewhat to Mr. Gray's dissatisfaction. He had gone in old days twice every Sunday with his father, and he preferred adopting the old habits to frequenting the chapel whither Mr. Gray desired to conduct him. Sometimes Mattie accompanied him; more often, when he knew his ground, he went by himself, leaving Mattie to her father's escort.

Meanwhile business slowly but surely increased; the connection extended—all went well with these three watchers—each watching for a different purpose, with an equal degree of earnestness.

.

END OF THE SIXTH BOOK.

BOOK VII.

SIDNEY'S GRATITUDE.

H

BOOK

CHAPTER I.

MAURICE HINCHFORD IN SEARCH OF HIS COUSIN.

NEARLY a year had passed away since the firm of
Hinchford and Gray started in business and aston-
ished the suburbs.   In search of that rising firm,
a young man, fresh from foreign travel, was wan-
dering in the outskirts of Peckham one February
night. A man who had crossed deserts, climbed
mountains, and threaded mountain passes with
comparative ease, but who was quickly lost in the
brick and mortar wilderness into which he had
ventured.

This man, we may say at once, was Maurice
Hinchford, a man who had seen life and spent a
fortune in an attempt to enjoy it.   A Sybarite,
who had wandered from place to place, from kingdom to kingdom, until even novelty had palled

H 2

upon him, and he had returned back to his father and his father's business. During this long holi-day he had thought much of his cousin Sidney, the man to whom he had taken no passing fancy, and whose life he had helped to blight—whom, by way of atonement, he had once wished to advance in the world.

Sidney Hinchford had been constantly before him during his pilgrimage ; before him that indignant figure which had repelled all excuse, on the night he reached his one and thirtieth year ; he could see it hastening away in the night shadows from the house to which it had been unsuspiciously lured.

On his return, not before, for he had wandered from place to place, and many letters had mis-carried—amongst them the missive which had told him of his uncle's death and cousin's blindness— he heard of the calamity which had befallen Sidney in his absence.

He had been ever a feeling man, and forgetting the past rebuff he had received—thinking, perhaps, that his cousin was in distress, he started at once

in search of him. To do Maurice Hinchford
justice, it was on the very day on which he had
reached London, and before he had seen his
mother and sisters. No assurance of his father
that Sidney was in good hands contented him ; he
must judge for himself. He had the Hinchford
impetus to proceed at once straightforwardly to
work ; he was a man who was sorry for the harm
he had done in his life—one of those comfortable
souls, who are always sorry *afterwards !*—a loose
liver, with a conscience that would not keep quiet
and let events flow on smoothly by him. He had
sobered down during his travels, too ; he had met
with many acquaintances, but no friends—in all
his life he had not found one true friend who
would have stood by him in adversity, and shared
his troubles, even his purse, with him.

Fortunately Maurice Hinchford had not known
adversity, and had shared his purse with others
instead. A rich man, an extravagant one, but a
man of observation, who knew tinsel from pure
gold, and sighed very often when he found himself
compelled, perforce, to put up with the tinsel. Life

such as his had wearied him of late; men of
his own class had sworn eternal amity, and then
laughed·at him when his back was turned; men of
a grade inferior had toadied him, cringed to him,
sponged upon him; women had flattered him for
his wealth's sake, not.loved him for his own—all
had acknowledged him one· of those good fellows,
of which society is always proud; but for *himself*
nobody cared save his own flesh and blood—he
could read that fact well enough, and its constant
reiteration·on the faces of "his set" annoyed him
more than he could have believed.

This favourite of fortune, then, annoyed with
society's behaviour, had started forth in search of
Sidney an hour after the news was learned from
his father's lips. He had a great deal to say
to Sidney; he had not entered into any explanations in that letter which Sidney had coolly responded to—he could say more *viva voce*; and now
the storm was more than a year old, his cousin
would surely put up with more, and listen to him.

But firstly, Maurice Hinchford had to find his
cousin; and having wandered from the right track,

it became a matter of some difficulty. He had strayed into a "new neighbourhood"—a place always famous for its intricacies—and he floundered about new streets, and half-finished streets, asking manifold questions of the aborigines, and receiving manifold directions, which he followed implicitly, and got lost anew in consequence.

· The stragglers were few and far between, and Maurice waited patiently for the next arrival— standing under a lamp-post at the corner of a street. He had given up all hope in his own resources, and had resolved to enlist the next nondescript in his service, be his terms whatever his rapacity dictated. But the next nondescript was a woman, and he was baffled again. A young woman in a great hurry, to whom he could not offer money, and whose progress he scarcely liked to arrest, until the horror of another vigil under that melancholy gas-lamp overcame his reluctance to intrude.

"I beg pardon," he said, hastily; "I am looking for Park Place. Will you oblige me, Miss, by indicating in which direction it may lie *now*?"

" As straight as you can go, sir."

" Ah! but, confound it, I can't go straight.
Not that I'm intoxicated," he said quickly, seeing
his auditor recoil, and make preparations for a
hasty retreat, "but these streets are incompre-
hensibly tortuous."

The listener seemed to look very intently towards him for an instant. The voice appeared to
strike her.

" Whom do you want in Park Place?" was the
quick answer.

" A Mr. Hinchford, of the business of Gray and
Hinchford."

" You are his cousin Maurice?"

" By George!—yes. How did you know that?"

" I guessed it—that's all."

" You are a shrewd guesser, Miss," he said.
" Yes, I am his cousin Maurice, and you are——"

" Mattie Gray, his partner's daughter."

" Oh ! indeed !"

" I have seen you once before—you brought
your father, some years ago, to a stationer's shop
in Great Suffolk Street."

"Right—a retentive memory."

"I seldom forget faces—it is not likely that I should have forgotten yours."

"Why not?"

"I have heard so much of you since then," was the answer, cold and cutting as the east wind that was swooping down the street that night.

"Oh! have you?"

Maurice walked on by her side; after a few moments Mattie said to him,

"What do *you* want with Sidney?"

"Many things. I am anxious to see him—very anxious."

"Your presence can but give him pain—why expose him to needless suffering by this intrusion?"

"I have a hope that it will not be considered an intrusion, Miss Gray," said Maurice, stiffly.

"I can see no reason why you should hope that."

"I am his relation—his——"

"Sir, I know what you are," said Mattie, sharply; "I know all your history, and all the harm you have done to him, and Harriet Wesden, and me."

"And you!—*and you*, Miss!" he repeated harshly.

"An evil action spreads evil in its turn, and there is no knowing where it may end, Mr. Hinchford," said Mattie; "yours affected my character."

"I don't see that—how was that possible?"

"Whilst you were playing your villain's trick on Harriet Wesden, I was searching the streets for her. I kept her secret after her return, and, therefore, could not give my employer a fitting reason for my absence from the business left in trust to me. I was discharged."

"I am very sorry," said Maurice, energetically; "upon my soul, I had no idea of all the harm my folly—my villainy, if you will—had caused till now! Miss Gray, you don't know how sorry I am !"

"I don't care."

"Is that merciful or womanly?"

"Perhaps not. But I will believe that you are sorry, if you will not accompany me further."

"Miss Gray, I must come. More than ever, I am resolved to see him to-night."

" Very well."

They went on together, both walking at a brisk pace, Maurice a little discomfited, and with his head bent down and his hands behind him.

"May I ask," he said after some moments' silence, " if he be well?"

" He is well."

" Blind still ?"

" Yes."

" May I ask you, as his friend, let me say, if his means be adequate to his support ?"

" Ah ! you have come to ask him that—to see that for yourself ?"

" Not exactly—it is one of many reasons."

" Keep that from him, then," cried Mattie; "spare him that humiliation."

" Why humiliation, Miss ?"

" It is humiliation, it is an insult, to offer help to the man whose life you have embittered. You that have known Sidney, worked with him in your office, professed to be his friend, should have fathomed that part of his character, at least, which is based upon his pride. Sir, I doubt if he esteem you very much, but he will certainly hate you if you talk of money."

"Then I'll not talk of it."

"And you'll not go back?"

"I never go back," said Maurice; "I'm a Hinch-ford."

"All the Hinchfords whom I have known have been honest, earnest men, striving to do good, and detesting cunning and disguise. I hope that you are the first that has disgraced the name."

"I hope so. Phew! how hot it is!"

Maurice Hinchford felt exceedingly uncomfortable under these continued attacks; still there was a novelty in all this dispraise and plain-speaking. A brusque young woman this, whose character interested him, and whose warmth in his cousin's service he respected, despite the darts with which she transfixed him.

He did not flinch from the purpose he had formed, however, He *was* anxious to see his cousin, to receive the attack in full, and defend himself; to prove to Sidney, if it were possible, that he was not quite the unprincipled villain that was generally supposed. So he kept on his way, and this first little dash of the waters of opposition against him did not affect him much. Mattie's energetic advice puzzled him, certainly; she spoke warmly in Sidney's cause—as if she were interested in him, and had a right to take his part—was there any reason for that brisk attack upon him, save her own outraged dignity at the slander which, by his means, had indirectly fallen upon her? He kept pace with her, but did not speak again. She was not inclined to reply with any "graciousness" to his questions; he saw that he had annoyed her already by the object of his mission, and that it was the better policy, the truer act of courtesy, to maintain a rigid silence.

Mattie spoke first.

"This is the house," she said, stopping before a shop already closed for the night. "You are still of the same mind?"

"Yes."

"You cannot do good here—you may do harm."

"Your pardon, but I am of a different opinion."

"Very well then."

Mattie gave a little impetuous tug to the bell; Ann Packet opened the door, and Mattie and her unwilling escort passed into the shop, the latter the object of immense attraction from the round-eyed, open-mouthed serving-maid. Events flowed on so regularly and monotonously in that quarter of the world, that the advent of a tall, well-dressed stranger, was a thing to be remarked, and, Ann Packet hoped, to be explained.

Mattie ran at once into the parlour, where her father was sitting over his work. He looked up with a bright smile as she entered.

" Where's Sidney, father ?"

" In his own room."

" Here is his cousin. Sidney must be prepared to see him, or to deny himself to him."

" What cousin is that ?" Mr. Gray asked, a little irrelevantly, being taken aback by the news.

Mattie explained, and ran up-stairs. Mr. Gray pushed aside the stone upon which he had been writing, turned up his coat-cuffs, and buttoned his black coat to the chin. He knew the story in which that cousin had played his part perfectly well; had he forgotten it, his remembrance of old faces would not have betrayed him in this instance. Here was the man to whom he had administered a fugitive lecture in the dead of night at Ashford railway station, once more before him; here was a chance of touching the heart of a most incorrigible sinner—a sinner worthy of *his* powers of conversion. He would tackle him at once; he would warn him of the errors of his ways, and of the infallible results of them, if he did not listen to the warning voice. He was just in the mood for delivering a sermon, and there was no time like the present. Now for it!

Mr. Gray turned the handle of the parlour door and skipped into the shop.

CHAPTER II.

MAURICE RECEIVES PLENTY OF ADVICE.

MAURICE HINCHFORD had been told by Mattie
to wait in the shop until she returned; and, obedient
to her mandate, he had taken his seat on a very
tall, uncomfortable stool, on which he could have
remained perched more at his ease had a balance-
pole been provided. Here he had remained, looking round the shop, and taking stock of its manifold contents—glancing askance now and then at
Ann Packet, whose curiosity was not entirely
satiated until Mr. Gray intruded on the scene.

At the first click of the door-handle, Maurice
looked round expecting to see his cousin, but was
disappointed by the presence of a small and agile
man in black, who leaped on to a second chair

beside him, and commenced nodding his head vigorously.

"Good evening, sir," said Maurice. "Mr. Gray, I presume?"

"We have met before, sir—my name *is* Gray."

"Really!—I do not remember——"

"Possibly not, sir; there are many unpleasant reminiscences we are always glad to escape from," said Mr. Gray. "I am connected with one. You and I met on the platform of the Ashford railway station, one winter's night, when Miss Wesden claimed my protection from a snare that had been laid for her."

"Oh!"

Maurice had dropped into a hornet's nest. Whom next was he to confront before his cousin Sidney came upon the scene?—from whom else was he to hear a sharp criticism on those actions of the past, which no one regretted more than he. Luck was against him that night.

"You remember me?" said Mr. Gray. "Before the train departed I gave you a little counsel for your future course in life—a warning as to whither

a persistence in your evil habits would lead you—
you remember?"

"Oh! yes—I remember."

"Have you taken that warning to heart?—I fear
not. Have you been any wiser, better, or more
honest from that day?—I fear not. Have you
not rather proceeded on your evil course, despising
the preaching of good men, the warning of God's
word, and gone on, on—down, down, without a
thought of the day when all your actions in this
life would have to be accounted for?"

Bang came Mr. Gray's hard hand on the
counter, startling Maurice Hinchford's nerves
somewhat, and causing innumerable articles in the
glass cases thereon to jump spasmodically with the
shock.

"I—" began Maurice.

"Don't interrupt me, sir—I will not be interrupted!—you have come hither of your own free
will, seeking us out, and fearing not the evidence
of our displeasure, and now, sir, you must hear
what is wrong in your acts, and what will be good

for your soul. Do you know, oh! sinner, that that soul is in deadly peril?"

" I know—"

" Sir, I will not be interrupted!" cried Mr. Gray again; "I am not accustomed to be interrupted when I am endeavouring to awaken a hardened conscience to a sense of its condition, and I will not be now. And I call upon you at this time— now is the accepted time, sir, now is the day of salvation—to amend, amend, amend! You have been a spendthrift, profligate, everything that is bad; you have studied yourself in every action of life, and neglected the common duties due to your neighbour as well as to your Maker. You have gone on smiling in your sinful course, heeding not the outcry of religious men against your hideous career, recking not of the abyss into which you must plunge, and on the brink of which, you—a man, with an immortal soul committed to your charge —are standing now! One step more, perhaps, one wilful step forward, and you are lost for ever. *Lost!*" he shouted, with the frenzy of a fanatic,

as well as the vehemence of a good man carried
away by his subject; and the shrill cry made the
glasses round the gas lamps ring again, and vibrated
unpleasantly through Maurice's system. This was
becoming unendurable.

"If you will allow me—" began Maurice.

"Sir, I will not be interrupted!" shouted Mr.
Gray, with more hammering upon the counter; "I
know what is good for you, and I insist upon a
patient hearing. You are a man in danger of destruction, and I cannot let you go blindfold into
danger, without bidding you stop whilst time is
mercifully before you. Let me divide the subject, in the first place, into three heads."

Maurice groaned inwardly, and stared at the
preacher. There was no help for it; there was no
escape. He might jump to the floor and fly for his
life; or he might tip up Mr. Gray's chair, upset that
gentleman, and then gag him; but neither method
would bring him nearer to that purpose for which he
had ventured thither; and until Sidney appeared
there was nothing to do but sit patiently under
the infliction and listen to the full particulars of

his dangerous state. He put his hands on his knees,
surveyed the speaker, and submitted; in all his life
he had never heard such a bad opinion of himself,
or listened to so sweeping a condemnation of all
his little infirmities. Mr. Gray ran on with great
volubility, pitching his voice unpleasantly high;
Maurice's blood curdled, once he was sure his hair
rose upon his head, and more than once cold water
running down the curve of his back bone could
not have more forcibly expressed the sensations of
the moment. And then those horrid bangs upon
the counter—always coming when least expected,
and going off like cannon shots in his ears; and the
gesticulatory flourishes, and the falsetto notes when
more than usually excited, and, above all, the un-
ceasing flow of invective and persuasion—an unin-
termittent shower-bath of the best advice, powerful
enough to swamp a congregation.

Maurice's head ached; his eyes watered; the
shop grew dizzy; the books and prints revolved
slowly round him; the ceiling might be the floor,
and the floor the ceiling, with the gas branch
screwed upside down in it, for what he knew of

the matter; he lost the thread of the discourse,
and found the heads thereof inextricably confused;
he understood that he was a miserable sinner—the
worst of sinners—or he should not be sitting there
with all those horrible noises in his ears; the
figure in the chair before him, heaved up and
down, moved its arms right and left, possibly
threw double summersaults; it was all over with
the listener—he was going silly, he scarcely knew
now with what object he had come thither—oh!
his head!—oh! this never-ending, awfully rapid
Niagara of words!

He made one feeble effort at resistance.

"Look here, old fellow—if you'll let me off—
I'll—I'll build a tabernacle," he burst forth; and
again that terrible "Sir, I will not be interrupted!"
stopped all further intrusion upon the subject of
discourse.

Mr. Gray was delighted with that subject, with
that listener—one of the finest specimens of iniquity
he had encountered for many years!—and he did
not think of stopping yet awhile. Where was the
hurry?—time, although valuable, could not be

better spent than on that occasion—his heart was
in the task he had set himself, and he would do his
very best!

Mattie came to the rescue at last; she had
been watching the delivery of the sermon for
some time over the parlour blind, informing Sidney, who had entered the parlour, of the energy
of the father, and the patient endurance· of his
cousin.

Disturbed as he had been by his cousin's arrival,
and undecided for some time as to the expediency
of granting him an interview or not, Sid could not
refrain from a smile at Maurice's unenviable position. He remembered Mr. Gray's first charge upon
his sins, and the unsparing length to which he had
extended his remarks upon them; he could imagine
the position of Maurice Hinchford at that juncture,
and realize the feelings with which that gentleman
heard and suffered.

"I think I'll go to him now, Sidney," said
Mattie.

It had been Sidney and Mattie—as between
brother and sister—for a long time now.

"Will your father admire the intrusion?" asked Sid, drily.

"Perhaps he *is* doing good," said Mattie, who regarded matters akin to this more seriously than the blind man ; "I'll wait a while."

And all this time Maurice was praying for help. It had not been a very pleasant idea, that of facing his cousin for the first time ; but now the thought occurred to him that he would rather face the very worst—even that obnoxious being, of whom the preacher earnestly warned him—than hear this man inveigh against his sins any more.

Mattie quietly entered the shop. The spell was broken; Mr. Gray paused with his right arm above his head—he was just coming down with another bang on the counter—and Maurice leaped off his stool, to which he had been transfixed, and shook hands violently with Mattie in his bewilderment.

"He will see me, Miss Gray?"

"Yes. If you wish it."

"Thank you—thank you ! Is he in the parlour?"

"Yes."

"And so be warned, young man—there is no ex-

cuse left you—not one, now. You have been
warned of all the evils which a guilty life incurs
upon those who go on their way defiantly!"

" Oh! yes—I have been warned, sir; there's not
a doubt of it—I'm afraid I have put you to a great
deal of trouble?" said Maurice, not yet recovered
from his confusion.

" In a good cause, I don't mind trouble."

" Very kind of you, I'm sure. In the parlour,
you said, Miss Gray?—then I'll go to him at once.
It must be getting very late."

Mr. Gray was proceeding to follow Maurice,
when Mattie touched him on the arm and arrested
his progress.

" I think we had better leave them together.
Their business is scarcely ours."

" What?—ah! exactly so, my dear. But I wish
you had not interrupted me quite so unceremoni-
ously—the impression I was making upon that
young man was wonderful! Great heaven! if it
is left for me to work his regeneration at the last,
how proud I shall be! Mattie, I think I have
moved him—he has already said something about

building a tabernacle, a chapel, or something; but I scarcely caught the words at the moment—think of that man, so wicked, and perverse, and designing, proceeding after all, in the straight and narrow way! It's wonderful!"

In the meantime, Maurice Hinchford had entered the parlour, closed the door behind him, and advanced towards the figure at the table, sitting in the full light of the gas above his head. Maurice paused and looked at him.

Sidney had changed; he was looking older; there was a thread or two of silver in the dark waving hair; and the eyes, which blindness had not dimmed, had that melancholy vagueness of expression, by which such eyes are always characterized.

" Well, Sidney—I am here at last."

" I am sorry that you have taken the trouble to call."

" Indeed !—why ?"

" I think you and I are best apart. We know each other far too well, by this time."

" Have patience with me, Sidney. I think not."

He drew a chair nearer his cousin, and sat down.

He had not offered to shake hands with Sidney; he felt that his cousin would have resented that attempt; that he was regarded as a man who had done a grievous wrong, and from whom no professions of friendship or cousinly regard would be received. He had come with a faint hope of doing good—in some way or other, he scarcely knew himself; of extenuating in some way—almost as indefinite to him—the past conduct which had placed him in so sinister a light.

"Sidney," he said, "I wish that you had accepted that invitation to meet me which I made you. I could have explained much."

"No explanation, Maurice, would have been satisfactory to me at that time."

"Will it be now, then?" he asked, eagerly catching at the words which implied possibly more than his cousin had wished to convey.

"I would prefer dismissing the subject altogether," Sid replied. "If you will tell me candidly and honestly that you are sorry for the past, I will be glad to hear it—and believe it."

"You bear me no malice, then?"

" No—I have outlived it."

" Then you will——"

" I will do nothing, but remain with those good friends who have taken pity on my helplessness," he said, sternly.

" Sidney, pray understand me. I don't wish you to think me a wholly bad man—God knows I am not that—I have never been that. I have had bad friends, evil counsellors, if you will—mine was never a resolute nature, but one easily led away from the first. I was an only son, spoiled by an indulgent father, spoiled by the money which was lavished on me, spoiled by the crowd which the spending of that money brought about me—nothing more."

" That is bad enough," said Sid.

"I own that. I own that I was flattered to my moral ruin, Sidney—that they, who called themselves my friends, cheered on that downfall, and made it easy to me—scoffing at all worlds purer than their own. I was young, vain, impressionable, and far from high-principled when I first met Harriet Wesden at Brighton."

"I would rather not hear the story," said Sidney, uneasily.

Maurice paid no heed to the remark, but went on hastily; and Sidney, suppressing his intention to arrest the narrative, sat still and listened to its weaknesses, its mystery, and yet its truth.

"Harriet Wesden was a romantic school-girl— a young woman who knew little of life, or had read the fictions, highly-coloured, concerning it, till she might have belonged to dream-land for the realities about her. She was led away by a senior scholar, too, as romantic as herself, and more designing; and she and I met, talked, corresponded—fell in love with each other."

"I deny that."

"Patience, Sidney! on my soul we did! I was not a villain, but a man led away by my vanity and this girl's preference for me, and I loved her. I don't say that it was a very true or passionate love; but it *was* a love, which burned fiercely enough for a time—which would have been purer and better, but for the evil counsellor and false friend who was always with me, to treat life, and love, and honour as a jest."

"The man I met at your house?"

"No. A man who has died since then—thank God, I was almost adding, for he worked me much evil, and death only freed me from him."

"Go on."

"When Harriet Wesden and I parted, I believe we truly loved each other. I had assumed a false name at the outset, and had maintained it throughout our strange courtship—fearing the discovery of governesses, and not knowing the character of her to whom my folly had lured me. I was to go abroad at my father's wish, and I left, fully resolving to write to her, and own all, and ask her if she would wait for me. Then came long absence, fresh scenes, new friends, new dissipations, a belief that she would easily forget me, being but a child when I had seen her last; and so the old, old story, varied scarcely from the many that have gone before it. Sidney, she did forget me—did discover that, after all, it was but a fleeting fancy of her own."

"No."

"I think the next part of my story proves that.

I met her again after an absence of a few years, in the streets, near her house in Suffolk Street, whither I had conducted my father to see yours. All my old passion for her revived—but it was a struggle with her to endure my presence at first. Still I was from the old days; I revived in her memory the one romance that had been hers—I had not played a false part therein, and could easily excuse my long silence. I found out the friends whom she visited in the neighbourhood of New Cross; I formed their acquaintance, and met Harriet Wesden more frequently. Her old assertion that she never wished to see me again— that she loved another, whose name she would never confess to me—wavered. I saw it, and, carried away by the impression created, I did my best to win her."

"Away from me?—well, you succeeded. She wrote to me at that time, confessing her inability to think of me longer as a lover."

"She wrote, not knowing her own mind, I believe. At that time she was disturbed in thought concerning us—she was often cold and repellent

to me, and it was difficult to understand her.
Well, Sid, throughout all this, I loved her."

"Why keep to your false name, then?"

"I was ready to confess the truth, at every interview; then I put off the avowal, after my old
fashion. I knew by that time that your father and
yourself were lodging at the stationer's shop, and I
formed a shrewd guess as to the rival I had in
her affections. Finally, Sid, there came that night
at New Cross, when she was carried away to Ashford. As I hope to be saved, I had no design
against her then; in good faith, I was her escort
to the railway station; it was only as we ap-
proached that station, that the ruse suggested
itself—that the devil whispered in my ear his
temptation. I knew the time of the mail-train; I
had been by it *en route* to Paris only a few weeks
since; I led her along, unsuspecting of evil, to
the other side of the railway station. She was
with me in the carriage before I became conscious of the heinousness of the act I had committed. Even then I intended her no harm; I
trusted all to circumstance; I was even prepared

to marry her, rather than lose her; I was under a spell, Sidney!"

"Yes—the spell of the devil."

"When she discovered the truth, I found that I had secured her hate, rather than her love; at Ashford station she faced me like a tigress, and, full of the honest indignation that possessed her, held me up to the shame I deserved before a host of people—pointed me out as a coward and knave who had sought to cruelly deceive her. She claimed the protection of that—that terrible man in the shop there—he was at Ashford as you know—and I was glad to hide my head in the railway carriage, and be borne away from his withering contempt. That's the story. I will not tell you of the sorrow which I experienced for the harm that I had done her—of the shame that has remained with me since then—of the turn which she even gave to my character. Sidney, I would have made any reparation in my power—but I was baffled and degraded, and dared not look upon her any more."

"That man I met at your house—he knew the story?"

"He knew the beginning of it; and for Harriet Wesden's sake—and to redeem her character in the mind of a man who has not a high estimate of women—I told the end."

Sidney sat and thought for a while. Then he pronounced his verdict.

" All this assures me that you are easily led away —that it is only chance that has kept you from being wholly a bad man. You are weak, vacillating, and unprincipled—you are no Hinchford."

"I have tried to do my best all my life, but somehow failed," said Maurice, ruefully; "impulse has led me wrong when my heart has meant right—candidly, cousin, I have been a fool more than once. But you cannot believe that I would do harm to any human being in cold blood?"

" Possibly not. But what virtue is there in that?"

"Let me add, Sidney, that I honestly believe that I have been altering for the better for the last two years. I have seen the emptiness of all my friends' professions; their greed of gain and love of self; have turned heart-sick at their evil-speaking, lying, and slandering. I feel that I haven't a friend; that I have 'used up' all the pleasures in the world, and that there is nothing I care for in it."

" Yours is a bad state, that leads to worse, as a rule, Maurice."

" I know it—I feel it."

" And you are truly sorry for all the harm that you have done us in life—Harriet, I, and others?"

" With all my heart—truly sorry."

" I can forgive you, then. I have been taught by good friends to be more charitable in my heart towards men's motives. A year ago, I thought I should have hated you all my life."

He held forth his hand, which Maurice took and shook heartily in his.

" Understand me," said Sidney, still coldly, " I forgive you, but I do not need your help, and your presence, under any circumstances, will always give me pain. We shall never be true friends—we shall respect each other better apart."

"Is it fair to think that? You who have heard me declaim against my vain and objectless life."

"Yours is a life to rejoice at, and to do good with, not to mourn over. Seek a wife, man, and settle down in your sphere, honoured by good men, and honouring good things."

"Ah! fair advice; but the wife will come for my money's sake, for the good things which *I* possess, and which she and her relations will honour in their way, with all their heart, and soul, and strength!"

"Timon of Athens!" said Sidney, almost satirically.

"Sidney, I would give up all my chances for one or two true friends. You don't know what a miserable wretch I am!"

"You will be better presently. You have seen too much life lately, and the reaction has rendered you *blasé*. Patience and wait. As for the wife——"

"Well?"

"Seek out Harriet Wesden again, and do her justice."

"But you——"

"She never loved me, Maurice; you were her first love, and her last. She is leading a life that is unfit for her, and you can make amends for all the shadows you have cast upon it."

"I could never face her."

"Then you are a greater coward than I thought."

"It's odd advice," he muttered; "seek out Harriet Wesden again! Oh! I know how that will end, and what 'good' will result from that. But *you* wish it?"

"Yes," said Sidney, after a moment's further reflection.

"And her address?"

Sidney repeated it; he took it down in his pocket-book, and then rose to depart.

"I am going now. I may trouble you once again, Sidney, if you will allow me."

"As you will—if you think it necessary."

Maurice Hinchford shuffled with his feet uneasily, keeping his eyes fixed on his blind cousin.

" May I ask," he said at last, " if—if you are happy here ?"

" Yes, as happy as it is possible for one in my condition to be."

" They are kind to you ?"

".Very kind."

" They are a sharp couple—father and daughter —they——"

" Oh! don't speak ill of them, Maurice; you do not know them, and cannot estimate them at their just worth."

" I might endure the daughter, for hers is a pleasant sharpness that one doesn't object to ; but, oh ! that dreadful vigorous little parson, or whatever he is."

" Good night," said Sidney, meaningly.

" One moment—I'm off in a minute now, Sid. There's one thing I did wish just to allude to— nothing about money, mind," he added hastily, noticing Sidney's heightened colour and proud face, and remembering Mattie's previous caution.

" What is it ?" asked Sidney.

" I did wish to say how sorry I was to hear of

the calamity, that had befallen you—that the bad news, which was told me to-day for the first time, has shocked me very much. But you'll not believe me —you still think I'm hard, cruel, and indifferent."

" No, I don't think that. But I don't care to dwell upon a painful topic."

" And about advice—what medical advice have you had, may I ask?"

" Not any."

" No advice !—why not?"

" I was told long ago that when blindness seized me, it would be irretrievable. I was warned of its approach by an eminent man, who was not likely to make a mistake."

" We are all liable to mistakes in life," said Maurice, "and it might happen——"

" Pray dismiss the subject, Maurice."

" I met with a foreign oculist in Paris—he was an Italian, I think—who——"

" Good night—good night," said Sidney, hastily; " when a man has been trying hard to teach himself resignation, it is not fair to disturb him with ideas like these."

" Your pardon, Sid—I am going at once. Good night."

" Good night."

Sidney did not extend his hand again, and Maurice made no attempt to part in a more friendly manner than they had met ; profuse civilities could do no good, and though Maurice had gained his cousin's forgiveness, he had not roused his respect, or won upon his sympathy.

He passed into the shop, and took up his hat that he had left there on the counter. Mr. Gray looked at him, as at a fine subject which adverse fate was to snatch away from his experiments.

" You are going, young man?"

" Yes, sir—I hope I have not put you or your daughter to any inconvenience."

" No, sir," was his reply, beginning to turn up the collar of his coat above his ears, " no inconvenience. You are a stranger to this neighbourhood, and I'll just see you in the straight way, if you'll allow me."

" Oh ! dear no, thank you," said the alarmed Maurice ; " I'm well up in the way now—I could not think of taking you away from home at this time of night—thank you, thank you!"

He seized his hat, dashed at the lock, wrenched open the door, and flew for his life down the dark streets—no matter whither, or how far out of his route, so that he escaped Mr. Gray's companionship.

Half an hour afterwards, he was at New Cross railway station—the scene of his old duplicity—arranging for a telegraphic message to a Dr. Bario, resident in Paris.

CHAPTER III.

A DECLARATION.

HARRIET WESDEN had settled down like the rest
of the world, that is, this little world wherein live
and breathe—at least we hope so—these characters
of ours.

She had settled down! Life had taken its
sombre side with her; the force of circumstances
had set her apart from those for whom her heart
yearned; she became bound more to this dull
home; disappointment had wondrously sobered
her; when her heart had been at its truest and
best, it had seemed as though the whole world had
turned against her, and misjudged her.

There was no romance in her after that; her
romance had begun early and died early—for her
share in it, she was heartily ashamed. To look

back upon that past, note her weakness, and whither it had led her, was to make her cheeks flush, and her bosom heave; in those sober after-days that had come to her, she could scarcely comprehend the past.

Women change occasionally like this—more especially women whose hearts are sound, but whose judgments have not always been correct. She had met deceit face to face; her own presence of mind had only saved her perhaps from betrayal; she had passed through a vortex—and, escaping it, the shock had sobered her for life.

Harriet Wesden turned "serious"—a very good turn for her, and for all of us, if we could only think so. Still, serious people—more especially serious young people—are inclined to dash headlong at religion, and even neglect home duties, duties to friends, and neighbours, and themselves, for religious ones. They verge on the extremes even in sanctity, and extremes verge on the ridiculous.

Harriet Wesden gave up life's frivolities, and became a trifle austere in her manner; she had found a church to her taste, and a minister to her taste—a minister who verged on extremes, too, and yet was one of the best-meaning, purest-minded men in the world.

Harriet Wesden became his model member of the flock, as he became her model shepherd. She lived for him, and his services, and the bran span new church he had built for himself in the square at the back. She missed never a service, week-days or Sundays; early prayers, at uncomfortable hours, when the curates were sleeping, and the pew-opener audibly snored—daily sermons, evening services, special services for special out-of-the-way saints, and Sunday services innumerable.

Let it be written here, lest our meaning be mis-interpreted, that Harriet Wesden had improved vastly with all this—was a better, more energetic, and devout woman. If she went *too often* to church —that is quite possible—if she were a trifle "high" and pinned her faith on decorations, if she thought the world all vanity and vexation of spirit, if she were a little proud of carrying outward and visible signs of her own inward and spiritual grace, if she

even neglected her father, at times—poor old Wesden, who sadly needed cheerful society now—still
the end was good, and she was at her best then.
Serious people *will* appear a little disagreeable to
people who are not serious—but then what do
serious people think of their mundane critics, or
care for them?

Harriet Wesden fancied that she had set herself
apart from the world—that its vanities and belong-
ings scarcely had power to arrest her steady upward
progress. It did not strike her that whilst she remained in the world, the sorrows, joys, and his-
tories of its denizens must have power to affect
her.

Sidney Hinchford had mistrusted her—the man
for whom she had been anxious to make sacrifices,
had refused them, and discredited their genuineness; her only friend, in whom she thought there
could not be a possibility of guile, had supplanted
her. From that hour let her set herself apart from
them; bear no ill-feeling towards them, but keep
to her new world. Her life was not their lives,
and they were best away from her. After that

set in more strongly the seriousness to which we have alluded, and all former trace of Harriet Wesden's old self submerged for good—and all.

Mattie and Harriet met at times; Mattie would not give up the old friend, the girl she had loved so long and faithfully. Despite the new reserve— even austerity—that had suddenly sprung up, Mattie called at regular intervals, took her place between Harriet and Mr. Wesden, and spoke for a while of the old times. Harriet's manner puzzled her, but there seemed no chance of an explanation of it. Her quick observation detected Harriet's new ideas of life's duties, and she did not intrude upon them, or utter one word by way of argument, or in opposition. It happened, sometimes, that Harriet would be absent during Mattie's visits—" gone to church," old Wesden would say, ruefully—and Mattie would take her place by the deserted father's side, and play the part of daughter to him till Harriet's return.

Harriet seldom spoke of Sidney Hinchford to our heroine—he did not belong to her diminished world; she flattered herself that there was no

thought of him, or of what might have been, to
perplex her with new vanities. When the name
of Sidney Hinchford intruded upon the subject
of discourse, she heard it coldly enough. She
was always glad to learn that Sidney was well, and
doing well; it had even been a relief to her to
know that the business, after a stand-still of some
months, had taken a turn in the right direction;
but, when all was well, what was there to agitate
her? If Sidney were ill, and needed her help, she
would have taken her place at his side, perhaps; if
Mattie were ill even—though in her heart she felt
that she did not love Mattie so well as formerly—
she would have devoted herself to her service; but
they were both well, living under the same roof
with Mattie's father, and all things had changed
so since Suffolk Street times.

Harriet was from home at her usual devotions,
and her father was endeavouring to amuse himself,
as he best might under the circumstances, when a
stranger, who preferred not to give his name, requested an audience of Miss Wesden. Miss Wesden not being at home, Mr. Wesden would do for

the nonce, and the stranger was, therefore, shown into the parlour.

The *ci-devant* stationer put on his spectacles, and looked suspiciously at the new comer. Mr. Wesden was a man of the world, and hard to be imposed upon. A man more nervous and irritable with every day, but having his wits about him, as the phrase runs.

" Good evening," said the stranger.

"Good evening," responded Mr. Wesden. "Ahem —if it's a subscription for anything, I don't think that I have anything to give away."

"My name is Hinchford—Maurice Hinchford— possibly better known to you by the unenviable *alias* of Maurice Darcy."

"Oh! you're that vagabond, are you?—well, what do you want? You haven't come to torment my daughter again?" he said, in an excited manner; " you've done enough mischief in your day."

" I am aware of it, sir—I come to offer every reparation in my power."

" We don't wan't any of that sort of stuff, Mr. Hinchford."

"It's late in the day to offer an apology—to attempt an explanation of my conduct in the past; but if you would favour me with a patient hearing, I should be obliged, sir."

"I've nothing better to do," said Mr. Wesden; "take a seat, sir."

Maurice Hinchford seated himself opposite Mr. Wesden, and commenced his narrative, disguising and extenuating nothing, but attempting to analyze the real motives which had actuated his past conduct—motives which had been a little incomprehensible, taken altogether, and were therefore difficult to make clear before an auditor, as we have seen in our preceding chapter.

Mr. Wesden rubbed the back of his ear, stared hard over Maurice's head at the opposite wall, till Maurice looked behind him to see what was nailed up there; wound up by an emphatic " Humph !" when Maurice had concluded.

"Therefore, you see I was not so very much to blame, sir—that is, that there were at least extenuating circumstances."

"Were they, though?"

" Why, surely I have proved that ?"

" Can't say you have—can't say that I plainly see it at all. But, then, I haven't so clear a head as I used to have—oh ! not by a long way !"

"I hope at least you understand that I am heartily ashamed of my past conduct ?"

" I am glad to hear that, sir."

" I have become a different man."

" Been in a reformatory, perhaps?" suggested Mr. Wesden.

" I have found my reformatory in the world."

" Lucky for you."

" And the fact is, that as I have always loved your daughter—as only my own wicked impulse turned your daughter's heart away from me, I have come from abroad with the hope of making all the restitution in my power, by offering her my hand and fortune !"

" Have you, though ?"

Mr. Wesden stared harder than ever at this piece of information. Maurice took another glance over his shoulder, and then commenced a second series of explanations, speaking of his position and means, two things to which Mr. Wesden had been never indifferent.

"I don't know that it would be a bad thing for her," said Mr. Wesden; "she never talked to me about her love affairs—girls never do to their fathers—and very likely I haven't understood her all this time."

"Very likely not."

"Perhaps it is about you, and not the other one that has altered her so much. Any nonsense alters a woman, if she dwells upon it."

"Ahem!—exactly so."

"You may as well wait till she comes in now," said Mr. Wesden: "that's business."

"Sir, I am obliged to you."

"If you don't mind a pipe, I'll think it over myself, and you need not talk any more just at present. We don't have much talk in this house, and you've rather *gallied* me, Mr. Hinchford."

"Any commands I will attend to with pleasure."

Maurice Hinchford crossed his arms and sat back in his chair to reflect upon all this; for a lover he was sad and gloomy—scarcely satisfied with the step which he had taken, and yet brought to it by his own conscience, that had been roused from its inaction by his cousin Sidney. Here a life had been shadowed by his means, and he thought that it was in his power to brighten it; here was good to be done, and he felt that it was his duty at least to attempt the performance of it. Mr. Wesden sat and smoked his pipe at a little distance from him, and revolved in his own mind the strange incident which had flashed athwart the monotony of daily life, and scared him with its suddenness. In Harriet he had probably been deceived, and it was this young man whom she had loved, and whose eccentric courses had rendered her so difficult to comprehend. All the past morbidity, the past variable moods, the fluctuations in her health, were to be laid to this man's charge, and it was well that he had come at last, perhaps. Harriet was a good daughter, an estimable girl, who loved her Bible, and did good to others, but she was not a happy girl. Sorrowful as well as serious, the holiness of her life had not brightened her thoughts or lightened her heart, and was not therefore true holiness, this old man felt assured. Behind the veil there had been something hidden, and it was rather Maurice Hinchford than his blind cousin who stood between her and the light.

"I think you have done right to come," said Mr. Wesden, after half an hour's deliberation.

" I think so, too," was the response.

At the same moment, a summons at the door announced Harriet Wesden's return.

" I'll open the door myself, and leave you to explain," he said ; "don't move."

Maurice felt tight about the waistcoat now ; the romance was coming back again to the latter days; the heroine of it was at the threshold waiting for him. This was a sensation romance, or the roots of his hair would not have tingled so!

Mr. Wesden opened the door for his daughter, and allowed her to proceed half-way down the narrow passage before he gave utterance to the news.

"There has been a visitor waiting for you these last two hours, Harriet."

"For me!" said Harriet, listlessly; and, dreaming

not of so strange an intrusion on her home, she turned
the handle of the door and entered the parlour.
Then she stopped transfixed, scarcely believing her
sight, scarcely realizing the idea that it was Maurice Darcy standing there before her in her father's
house.

Maurice had risen.

"I fear that I have surprised you very much,
Miss Wesden," said he, hoarsely; "that possibly
this was not the best method of once again seeking
a meeting with you, This time with your father's
consent, at least."

"Sir, I do not comprehend; I cannot see
that any valid reason has brought you to this
house."

"I think it has—I hope it has."

"Impossible!"

"Miss Wesden, I have been relating a long
story to your father—may I beg you to listen to me
in your turn?"

"If it relate to the past, I must ask you to excuse me," was the cold reply.

"My guilty past it certainly relates to—I pray

you for an honest hearing. Ah! Miss Wesden,
you are afraid of me, still."

" Afraid!—no, sir."

Harriet Wesden looked at him scornfully, with
a quick, almost an impatient hand removed her
bonnet and shawl, and then passed to her father's
seat by the table, standing thereat still, by way
of hint as to the length of the interview. She
was more beautiful than ever; more grave and
statuesque, perhaps, but very beautiful. It was
the face that he had loved in the days of his wild
youth, and it shone before him once again, a
guiding star for the future stretching away beyond
that little room.

He would have spoken, but she interrupted
him.

" Understand me, Mr. Darcy—Mr. Hinchford,
I may say now, I presume—I wish to hear no excuses for the past, no explanations of your wilful
conduct therein—I have done with that and you. If
you be here to apologize, I accept that apology, and
request you to withdraw. If matters foreign to
the past have brought you hither, pray be speedy,

and spare me the pain of any longer interview than necessary."

"Miss Wesden, I must, in the first place, speak of the past."

"I will not have it!" cried Harriet, imperiously; "have I not said so?"

The minister round the corner would have rubbed his eyes with amazement at the fire in those of his neophyte. He would have thought the change savoured too strongly of the earth from which he and her, and other high-pressure members of his flock, had soared just a little above—say a foot and a half, or thereabouts.

"It is the past that brings me back to you, Harriet—the past which I would atone for by giving you my name and calling you my wife. I have been a miserable and guilty wretch—I ask you to raise me from my self-abasement by your mercy and your love?"

He moved towards her with all the fire of the old love in his eyes—those eyes which had bewildered her like a serpent's, in the old days. But the spell was at an end, and there was no power to bring her once more to his arms. She recoiled from him with a suppressed scream; her colour went and came upon her cheeks; she fought twice with her utterance before she could reply to him.

"Mr. Hinchford, you insult me!"

"No, not that."

"You insult me by your shameless presence here. I told you half a minute ago that I forgave you all the evil in the past. *I don't forgive it*—no true woman ever forgave it yet in her heart. I hate you!"

The minister round the corner would have collapsed at this, as well he might have done. Only that evening had he begged his congregation to love their enemies, and return good for evil, and Harriet Wesden had thought how irresistible his words were, and how apposite his illustrations. And fresh from good counsel, this young woman who had been unmoved for twelve long months, and during that time been about as animate as the Medicean Venus, now told her listener there that she hated him with all her heart!

" Enough, Miss Wesden. I have but to express

my sorrow for the past, and take my leave. Forgive at least the motive which has led me to seek
you out again."

" One moment—one moment !" said Harriet.

She fought with her excitement for an instant,
and then with a hand pressed heavily upon her
bosom, to still the passionate throbbing there, she
said :

" You must not go till I have explained also ;
you have sought out a girl whose young life you
cruelly embittered by your perfidy—let her explain something in defence. Mr. Hinchford, I
never loved you—as I stand here, and as this may
be my last moment upon earth, I swear that I never
loved you in my life ! There was a girl's vanity,
in the first place—almost a child's vanity, fostered
by pernicious teaching of frivolous companions—
afterwards there was a foolish romantic incertitude
—vanity still perhaps—that led me to trust in you,
and to give up one who loved me, and for whom I
ought to have died rather than have deserted—but
there was no love ! I knew it directly that I
guessed your cowardice, for I despised you utterly

then, and understood the value of the prize, my own misconduct had nearly forfeited. I was a weak woman, and you saw my weakness, and hastened to mislead me; but the wrong you would have done me taught me what was right, and, thank God! I was strong enough to save myself! There, sir, if only to have told you this, I am glad that you have sought an interview. Now, if you are a gentleman—go!"

He hesitated for an instant, as though he could have wished, even in the face of her defiance, to tell his story for the third time; then he turned away, and went slowly out of the room, defeated at all points, his colours lowered and trailing in the dust. Outside he found Mr. Wesden, standing with his back to the street door, smoking his pipe, and regarding the hall mat abstractedly. He looked up eagerly as Maurice Hinchford advanced.

"Well?—well?" he asked feverishly.

"Yes, it is well," was the enigmatic and gloomy answer; "I see what a fool I have been, Mr. Wesden. I know myself for the first time—good evening."

Mr. Wesden opened the door for him, and he passed out; the old man watched him for a while, and then returned to his favourite chair in the back parlour.

Harriet ran to him as he entered, and flung her arms round his neck.

"I have you to love, and look to still. Not quite alone—even yet!"

CHAPTER IV.

MORE TALK OF MARRIAGE AND GIVING IN MARRIAGE.

MAURICE HINCHFORD passed away from this story's scene of action. Suddenly and completely he disappeared once more, and they in the humble ranks of life knew nothing of his whereabouts. From Paris his father had received a letter that perplexed and even irritated him, for it was mysterious, and the head of the house of Hinchford detested mystery.

"I have run over here for a week or two—perhaps longer, perhaps less, according to circumstances," Maurice wrote; "you who are ever indulgent will excuse this flitting, which I will account for on my return. If anything calls for my

especial attention at the bank, telegraph to me, and
I will come back."

No especial business was likely to demand
Maurice's return; the bank went on well without
him, good man of business as he was when he set
his mind to it. His father's indulgence excused
the flitting, though he shook his head over his son's
eccentricity, after the receipt of the incomprehensible epistle. "Another of those little weaknesses
to which Maurice had been subject," thought the
indulgent father; "time he grew out of them now,
and married and settled, like other young men of
his age. If he would only sow his wild oats, what
an estimable man and honoured member of society
he would be. Poor Maurice!"

Sidney Hinchford, who, from his cousin's hints, had
anticipated a second visit from Maurice, felt even a
little disappointed at his non-appearance. Sidney
was curious; he would have liked to know the result of Maurice's proposal to Harriet Wesden, but
he kept his curiosity to himself, and did not even
mention to Mattie the advice which he had be-
stowed upon his cousin. He knew how the matter

had ended well enough; Maurice was in earnest, and would beat down all doubts of his better nature developing itself at last; the old love-story would be resumed, and all would go merry as a marriage bell with those two. He congratulated himself upon having done some good even at the eleventh hour, in having helped to promote the true happiness of the girl he had once loved.

Once loved!—yes, he was sure that passion belonged to the past; that it had died out of inaction, and left him free to act. He was not happy in his freedom; his heart was growing heavier than ever, but he kept *that* fact back for his friends' sakes, and was, to them, a faint reflex of the Sidney Hinchford whom they had known in better days.

He fell no longer into gloomy reveries; he took part in the conversation of the hour; there came, now and then, a pleasant turn of speech to his lips, a laugh with him—the old rich, hearty laugh— was not a very rare occurence; he believed himself resigned to his affliction, content with his position, and, for many mercies that had been vouchsafed unto him, he was truly grateful.

How to show his gratitude did not perplex him; he had made up his mind after Ann Packet had given him a piece of hers—he had watched for words, signs, sighs—he was only biding his time to speak. But he remained in doubt; it was difficult to probe to the depths; he was a blind man, and far from a clever one; he could only guess by sounds, and test all by Mattie's voice, and he was, therefore, still unsettled.

He resolved to end all, at last, in a quiet and methodical manner, befitting a man like him. He was probably mistaken; he had no power to make any one happy; his confession might dissolve the partnership between Mr. Gray and himself—for how could Mattie and he live in the same house together after his avowal and rejection?

But he had made up his mind, and he went to work in his old straightforward way one evening when Mattie was absent, and Mr. Gray was busy at his work beside him.

"Mr. Gray," said he, "I want to bespeak your sole attention for a few minutes."

"Certainly, Sidney," was the reply. "Shall I put my work away?"

"If you do not mind, for awhile."

" There, then !"

Sidney was some time beginning, and Mr. Gray said—

" It's about the business—you're tired of it ?"

" On the contrary, I am pleased with it, and the work it throws in *my* way. But don't you find me a little bit of a nuisance always here ?"

" You know better than that. Next to my daughter, do you hold a place in my heart."

" Thank you. Now, have you ever thought of me marrying ?"

" Of *you* marrying !" he echoed, in a surprised tone, that was somewhat feigned. " Why, whom are you to marry, Sid ?"

" Mattie, if she'll have me."

The lithographer rubbed his hands softly together—it was coming true at last, this dream of Mattie and his own !

" If she'll have you !" he echoed, again. " Well, you must ask her that."

" Do you think she'll have me—a blind fellow like me ? Is it quite right that she should, even ?"

"I don't know—I have often thought about that," said Mr. Grey, forgetting his previous expression of astonishment. "I don't see where the objection is, exactly, Sidney. You're not like most blind men, dulled by your affliction —and Mattie is very different from most girls. If she thought that she could do more good by marrying you, make you more happy, she would do it."

"I don't want a sacrifice—I want to make her happy," said Sidney, a little peevishly. "If she could not love me, as well as pity me, I wouldn't marry her for all the world."

"You must ask her, young friend—not me, then."

"But you do not refuse your consent?"

"No. My best wishes, young man, for your success with the dearest, best of girls. I," laying his hand on Sidney's shoulder for a moment, "don't wish her any better husband."

Sidney had not exhibited any warmth of demeanour in breaking the news to Mr. Gray; many men might have remarked his quiet way of entering upon the subject. But Mr. Gray was of a

quiet, unworldly sort himself, and took Sidney's
love for granted. How was it possible to know
Mattie, to live beneath the same roof with her, and
not love her very passionately?

"I think—mind, I only think—that Mattie will
not refuse you, Sidney," said Mr. Gray; "she
understands you well, and knows thoroughly your
character. It's an unequal match, remembering
all the bye-gones, perhaps—but you are not likely
to taunt her with them, or to think her any the
worse for them, knowing what she really is in
these days, thanks to God!"

"Taunt her!—good heaven!"

"Hush! that's profane. And the match is not
very unequal, considering the help you need—and
what a true comforter she will be to you. We
Grays are of an origin lost in obscurity; you Hinchfords come of a grand old stock—you don't consider this?"

"Not a bit."

"Nor I; but then, men who don't spring
from old families are sure to say so. I'm not
particularly struck with the advantages of hav-

M 2

ing possessed a forefather who came over with
the Conqueror. William the Norman brought
over a terrible gang of cut-throats and robbers, and
there's not a great deal to one's credit in being connected with that lot."

Sidney laughed.

"I never regarded it in that light before. What
an attack on our old gentility!"

"Gentility will not be much affected, Sidney.
Have you anything more to tell me?"

"Nothing now."

"Not that if you marry Mattie, the crabbed,
disputatious local preacher may stop with you?"

"I hope he will. He has been a good friend to
me, and will keep so, for his daughter's sake."

"And for your own, young man. I'll go back
to my work now."

But the work was in his way after that, and all
the effects of his strong will could not make it endurable. Sidney's revelation had disturbed his
work; he would try a little silent praying to himself—a selfish prayer he felt it was, and therefore
no sound escaped him—that this choice of Sid-

ney's might bring comfort and happiness to his daughter and himself.

He was sitting with his large-veined hands spread before his face, and Sidney was wrapt in thoughts of the change that might be in store for him, when Mattie knocked at the door.

"Sit here—I shan't come back yet awhile. We may as well end this part of the business at once."

Mattie entered, found her father busy behind the counter with his stock, said a few words, and passed into the parlour.

It was a second version of the proceedings at Camberwell. The father holding aloof, and giving suitor and maiden fair play.

CHAPTER V.

MATTIE'S ANSWER.

SIDNEY HINCHFORD heard the door open, and knew that the end was come. In a few minutes was to be decided the tenor of his after-life. He did not move, but remained with his hands clasped upon the table—a grave and silent figure in the lamp-light.

"What makes you so thoughtful to-night, Sid?"

The more formal Mr. Sidney had been dropped long since; Mattie had resisted the encroachment as long as it was in her power, but the friendship between them had been increased as well as their intimacy, and the more familiar designation was the more natural of the two.

"Am I looking very thoughtful, then, Mattie?"

"Oh!. so cross and black!"

"Black?—eh!" he repeated; "that's a singular colour to seize upon a man's countenance, when he is agitated and hopeful. Come and sit here by my side, Mattie, and hear what news I have wherewith to startle you."

"Not bad news?" she asked.

"You shall judge."

Mattie guessed the purport of the news, and there had been no necessity for her last query. She knew all that was coming now, and so prepared herself for a revelation that she had seen advancing months ago. Months ago, she had wondered how she should act on this occasion, what manner she should adopt, and in what way reply to him? She had rehearsed it in her mind, with fear and trembling, and tear-dimmed eyes; she had dreamed of it, and been very happy in her dreams; and now at last she was at fault, and her resources not to be relied on. Very pale, with her mind disturbed, and her heart throbbing, she took her place by his side, shawled and bonneted as she was, and waited for the end.

Sidney broke the ice.   The first few words faltered somewhat on his lip, but he gathered nerve as he proceeded, and finally related very calmly—almost too calmly—and plainly, the state of his feelings towards her.

"Your father and I have been speaking of you during your absence; I have suggested to him a change of life for myself and you—if you will only consent to sacrifice a life for my sake!   A selfish, and an inconsiderate request, Mattie, which I should not have thought of, had I not fancied that it was in my power to make you a good husband, a true and faithful husband, and to love you more dearly as a wife than friend.   But always understand, Mattie, that on your side it will be a sacrifice—that no after-repentance, only my death, can relieve you from the incubus—that for life you are tied to a blind man, and that all natural positions of life are reversed, when I ask you to be my guide, protector, comforter!   Always remember, too, Mattie, that without me you will be free, and your own mistress; you, a young woman, to whom will come fairer and brighter chances!"

It was an odd manner of proposing; possibly Mattie thought so herself, for she raised her eyes from the ground, and looked at him long and steadily.

"Sidney, have you well reflected on this step?" she asked.

"I have."

"Thought well of the sacrifice of all the past hopes you have had?—of the *incubus* that I may be to you some day—that without me you will be free, and your own master—you, to whom the fairer, brighter chance may come, when too late! Sidney, we know not what a day may bring forth!"

"My fate is in your hands, Mattie."

"What I have been, you know—you must have thought of lately. What I am now, a poor, plain girl, self-taught and homely, who may shame you with her ignorance—you know too. Sidney, I have dwelt upon this lately—until this night, now I am face to face with the truth, I thought that I had made up my mind."

"To refuse me?"

"No—to accept you. To be your loving wife

through life, aiding you, and keeping you from harm; but, now I shrink back from my answer!"

"Ah!" he said, mournfully; "it is natural."

"Not for my own sake," she added, quickly, "but for yours! For your happiness, not mine! Sidney, you have *not* settled down; you are not resigned to this present lot in life; there is a restlessness which you subdue now you are well and strong, but which may defeat you in the days to come. Years hence, I may be a trouble to you, a regret—you, a gentleman's son, and I—a stray! I may have made amends for my past life, but I cannot forget it; there will come times when to you and me the memory may be very bitter yet!"

"No, no!"

"Sidney, when I was that neglected child, I think I had a grateful heart; for I appreciated all the kindness that helped me upwards, and turned me from the dangerous path I was pursuing. I did not forget one friend who stretched his helping hand towards me—I have remembered them all in my progress, the agents of that good God, whose will it was that I should not be lost! Sidney, I would

marry you out of gratitude for that past, if I
honestly believed you built your happiness upon
me; but I could not let you marry *me* out of gratitude, or think to make me happy by a share of
affection that had no real existence. I would do
all for you!" she said, vehemently; "but you must
make no effort to raise *me* from any motives but
your love!"

Sidney started—coloured. Had he misunderstood Mattie until that day?—was he the victim of
his own treacherous thoughts after all?—the dupe
of an illusion which he had hoped to foster by believing in himself?

"Sidney, I will be patient and wait for the love
—hope in it advancing nearer and nearer every
day—strive for it even, if you will, and it lies in my
power. But I am above all charity."

"Mattie, you are not romantic? You do not
anticipate from me, in my desolate position, all the
passionate protestations of a lover? You will believe that I look forward to you as the wife in
whom alone rests the last chance of happiness for
me?"

"We cannot tell what is our last chance," said Mattie; "it is beyond our foresight—God will give us many chances in life, and the best may not have fallen to your share or mine. Sidney, there *was* a chance of happiness for you once—on which you built, and in which you never thought of me—do you regret that now?" she asked, with a woman's instinctive fear that the old love still lingered in his heart.

"Mattie, I regret nothing in the past. And in the future, I am hopeful of your aid and love. Can I say more?"

"Sidney," said Mattie, after a second pause, "I will not give you my answer to-night—I will not say that I will be your wife, for better for worse, until this day month. It is a grave question, and I ought not to decide this hastily. I must think— I *must* think!"

"Ah! Mattie, you don't love me, or it would be easy enough to say 'Yes,'" said Sidney.

"No, not easy."

"I can read my fate—eternal isolation!" he said gloomily.

"Patience—you can trust me; let me think for

a while if I can trust in you. You do not wish my unhappiness, Sid?"

"God forbid!"

"We have been good friends hitherto—brother and sister. For one more month, let us keep brother and sister still; there is no danger of our teaching ourselves to love one another less in that period. In that month will you think seriously of me—not of what will make me happy—but what will render *you* happy, as the fairy books say, for ever afterwards? Remember that it is for ever in this life, and that I am to sit by your side and take that place in your heart which you had once reserved for another—think of all this, and be honest and fair with me."

"I see. You distrust my love. You have no faith in my stability."

"I say nothing, Sidney, but that I feel it would be wrong to answer hastily. Are you offended with my caution?"

"No—God bless you, Mattie!—you are right enough."

"This day month I will take my place at your

side, and give you truly and faithfully my answer. It is not a long while to wait—we shall have both thought more intently of this change."

She left him, to begin his thoughts anew; her reply had disturbed his equanimity; he neither understood Mattie nor himself just then. What had perplexed him?—what had come over the spirit of his dream to trouble his mind, or conscience, in so strange a manner?

Mattie went to her room and locked the door upon her thoughts, upon that new wild sense of happiness which she had never known before, and which, despite the character she had assumed— yes, assumed!—she could not keep in the background of that matter-of-fact life, now vanishing away from her. She knew that she had acted for the best in giving him time to think again of the nature of his proposition—in restraining that impulse to weep upon his shoulder, and feel those strong arms enfolding her to his breast. The old days had startled her when he had spoken in so firm and hard a manner; that figure of the past which had been all to him flitted there still, and held her back, and stood between herself and him, despite the new happiness she felt, and which no past could wholly scare away.

She believed in her own coming happiness; that he would love her better for the delay—understand more fully why she hesitated. When the time came to answer " Yes!" she would explain all that had perplexed her, arrested her assent midway, and filled her with the fears of his want of love for her, his future discontent when irrevocably bound to her. Twice in life now he had offered his hand in marriage; twice had the answer been deferred, for reasons unakin to each other. It was singular; but this time all would end happily. He would love her with his whole heart, as he had loved Harriet Wesden, and she would be his proud and happy wife, cheering his prospects, elevating his thoughts, doing her best to throw across his darkened life a gleam or two of sunshine, in which he might rejoice.

She was very happy—for the doubts that had kept her answer back, went farther and farther away as she dwelt upon all this. There was a restless beating at her heart, which robbed her of calmness for awhile, but it was not fear that precipitated its action, and the noises in her ears might be the distant clash of marriage bells, which she had never dreamed would ring for him and her!

END OF BOOK THE SEVENTH.

BOOK VIII.

MORE LIGHT.

CHAPTER I.

A NEW HOPE.

WHETHER Sidney Hinchford gave much ulterior
thought to his proposal, is a matter of some doubt.
He had made up his mind before his conversation
with Mr. Gray and daughter, and had there been
no real love in his heart, he would not have drawn
back from his offer. His life apart from business was akin to his business life in *that;* reflection on what was best, just and honourable,
and then his decision, which no adverse fate was
ever afterwards to shake. He did not believe
in any motive force that could keep him from
a purpose—it was a vain delusion, unworthy of a
Hinchford!

On the morning of the following day, the cousin
of whom he had thought more than once entered

N 2

again upon the scene of action ; at an early hour,
when Mattie was busy in the shop, and Mr. Gray
was absent on a preaching expedition. Maurice
Hinchford's first inquiry was if Mr. Gray were
within, and very much relieved in mind he appeared
to be upon receiving the information that that
formidable Christian was not likely to be at home
till nightfall. Maurice did not come unattended ;
he brought a friend with him, whom he asked to
wait in the shop for awhile, whilst he exchanged
a few words with Sidney.

Mattie looked at the stranger, a tall, lank man,
with an olive face, and long black hair, which he
tucked in at the back between his coat and waistcoat in a highly original manner. He was a man
who took no interest in passing events, but sat "all
of a heap" on that high chair which had been
Maurice Hinchford's stool of repentance, carefully
counting his fingers, to make sure that he had not
lost any coming along.

"Good morning, Sidney," said Maurice, on
entering. "Not lost yet, old fellow!"

"Good morning, Maurice."

"I have brought the latest news—I have been abroad since my last visit here."

"Abroad again?"

"I'll tell you about that presently. If you're not too busy this morning, and I'm not too unwelcome an intruder, I should be glad to inform you how I fared by following your advice."

"You are not unwelcome, Maurice, though I cannot say that there is any great amount of pleasure experienced by your visit to me."

"Still cold—still unapproachable, after forgiving all the past!"

"But not forgetting, Maurice. You bring the past in with you—I hear it in every accent of your voice; all the figures belonging to it start forth like spectres to dismay me."

"Your past has no reproaches—what is it to mine?"

"A regret is as keen as a reproach."

"Ah! you regret the past!—some act in it, perhaps?" said Maurice, with curiosity.

"We should scarcely be mortal if we could look back without regrets, I think."

" Ah! but what is the keenest—bitterest?"

" That is a leading question, as the lawyers say."

" Then I'll not press it—I'll speak of my own regrets instead. I regret having followed your advice, Sidney."

" We are all liable to err—I meant it for the best."

" I called the following evening on Harriet Wesden—I offered her my hand, as an earnest of that affection which only needed her presence to revive again—I asked pardon for my past, and spoke of my atonement in the future. Could I do more ?"

" No."

Sidney was nervously anxious to learn the result, but he merely compressed his lips, and waited for the sequel. He would not ask how this had ended —his pride held back his curiosity.

" And she refused me, as you and I might have expected, had we more seriously considered the matter. By George, I shall never forget her fiery eyes, her angry gestures, her contempt, which seemed

withering me up—I knew that it was all over with
every shadow of hope, then."

" A man should never despair."

" It would be difficult to help it in the face of
that clincher, Sidney. Well, it served me right;
I might have expected it; I might have guessed
the truth, had I given it a moment's thought; but I
put my trust in you, Sidney, and a nice mess I have
made of it! Upon my honour, I would rather bear
two—say three—of Mr. Gray's sermons, than face
Harriet Wesden again."

" Still, you should not be sorry at having offered
all the reparation in your power."

" Well, now I come to think of it, Sidney, I'm
not sorry. To confess the real plain truth, I'm
glad."

" Indeed !"

" Because I have made a discovery, and if you're
half a Hinchford, you'll profit by the hint. Harriet
Wesden loves *you*."

Sidney's hands grappled the arms of his chair,
in which he half rose, and then set down again.
The red blood mounted to his face, even those

dreamy eyes flashed fire again—the avowal was too decided and uncompromising not to affect him.

"I do not wish to dwell upon this topic."

"Ah! but I do. It has been bothering me all the way to Paris—all the way back. I have been building fancy castles concerning it. I have been one gigantic, unmitigated schemer since I saw you last, planning for a happiness which is yours by a word, and which you deserve, Sid Hinchford. I feel that your life might be greatly changed, and that it is in your power to effect it."

"Were it my wish, it is too late. As it is not my wish—as I do not believe you," he added, bluntly—"as I have outlived my youthful follies, and am sober, serious, and unromantic—as I have made my choice, and know where my happiness lies, I will ask you not to pain me—not to torture me, by a continuance of this subject."

"Let me just give you a sketch of what she said to me."

"I will hear no more!" he cried, with an impatient stamp of his foot.

"I have done," said Maurice; "subject deferred

sine die—or tied round the neck with a big stone, and sunk for ever in the waters of oblivion. By George, Sid, that's a neat phrase, isn't it?—only it reminds one of drowning a puppy. And now to business."

" What more?" asked Sidney, curtly.

His cousin had annoyed him; stirred up the acrimony of his nature, and destroyed all that placidity of demeanour which he had fostered lately. He felt that he rather hated Maurice Hinchford again ; that his cousin was ever a dark blot in the landscape, with his robust health, loud voice, and self-sufficiency. This man paraded his own knowledge of human nature too obtrusively, and spoke as if his listener was a child ; he professed to have discerned in Harriet Wesden an affection for the old lover to whom she had been engaged—as if he, Sidney Hinchford, had been blind all his life, or was morally blind then ! Sidney would be glad to hear the last of him—to be left to himself once more ; his cousin was an intrusion—he desired no further speech with him, and he implied as much by his last impatient query.

"It's something entirely new, Sidney, and therefore you need not fear any old topics being intruded on your notice. I have brought a friend to see you."

"Take him away again."

"No, I'd rather not, thank you," was the aggravating response; "I made my mind up to bring him, and he's waiting in the shop."

"Maurice—you insult me!"

"Pardon me, cousin, but the end must justify the means. He has come from Paris to see you; he would have been here before, had not illness prevented him."

"Who is this man?"

"The cleverest man in Europe, I'm told—an eccentric being, with a wonderful mine of cleverness beneath his eccentricity. A man who has made the defects of vision his one study, and has become great in consequence. Sidney, you must see him!"

"You bring him here at your own expense, to inspect a hopeless case; you will shame me by being beholden to you—to you, of all men in the world!"

"I thought we had got over the past—forgiven it?"

"Yes, but——"

"But it can't be forgiven, Sid Hinchford, if you hinder me making an effort to atone to you in my way."

"With your purse?" was the cold reply.

"No; with my respect for you—my regret for a friend whom I have lost."

"A strange friend!"

"And I have faith in this man. I remember a case similar to yours, which——"

"Stop! in the name of mercy, Maurice—this cannot be borne at least. I am resigned to despair, but not to such a hope as yours. Let him come in, and laugh at you for your folly in bringing him hither."

"Bario!" called Maurice.

The lank man came into the parlour, set his hat on a chair, and looked at Sidney very intently. His vacuity of expression vanished, and a keen intelligence took its place.

"Good morning, sir," he said, in fair English;

"you are the blind gentleman Mr. Hinchford has requested me to see?"

"The same, sir."

"You are sure you're blind?"

"Maurice, this man is a——"

"Yes, very clever. You have heard of Dr. Bario—he has been resident in Paris some years now."

"Ah!" said Sidney, listlessly.

"There is a blindness that be not blindness, sir —that's my theory," said the Italian; "a something that comes suddenly like a blight—the off-spring of much excitement, very often."

"Mine had been growing upon me for years—I was prepared for it by a man as skilful as yourself."

"May I put to you his name."

Sidney told him, and Dr. Bario gave his shoulders that odious French shrug which implies so much. Such is the jealousy of all professions—extending even to the disciples of the healing art. A never thinks much of B, if he be jumping at the same prize on the bay-tree—Dr. Bario had his weak-ness.

"He might have mistaken the disease, and into this have half frightened you. People, odd mistakes do make at times—I myself have not been infallible."

"Possibly not," said Sidney, drily.

"In my youth of course," said the vain man, "when I listened a leetle too much to the opinions of others—it was once my way."

Sidney thought the speaker had altered considerably since then, but kept his idea to himself. He was endeavouring to be cool, and uninfluenced by this man's remarks; but they had set his heart beating, and his temples painfully throbbing. He was a fool to feel unnerved at this; it was a false step of his cousin's, and had given him much pain —but Maurice had meant well, and he forgave him even then.

"Do you mind turning just one piece more to the light?" asked the doctor.

Sidney turned like an automaton. Maurice drew up the back parlour blind; the doctor bent over his patient, and there was a long silence —an anxious pause in the action of three lives, for the doctor's interest was as acute as the cousin's.

"Well?" Maurice ejaculated at last.

"There's a chance, I think."

"A chance of sight!" cried Sidney; "do you mean that?—is it possible that you can give me hope of that—now?"

"I don't give hope, sir," said Dr. Bario; "it's a chance, that's all—everything. It's one nice case for *me*—not you, young man."

"What do you mean?"

"There's danger in it—it's light, death, or madness! I do not you advise to risk this—but there's one chance if you do!"

"*I will chance it!*"

He was not content with the present, then; it had been a false placidity—he would risk his life for light; life without it, even with Mattie, did not seem for an instant worth considering!

"Very good. To-morrow I will you send for—you will have to place yourself entire under my direction for more weeks than one, before the final operation be attempted."

"I agree to everything—may I accompany you now?"

"To-morrow," was the answer again.

"Oh! it will never come. Maurice," he said, offering his hand, "however this ends, I am indebted to you."

"Yes—but—but if it end badly?"

"It will be God's will."

"And if it end as I hope and trust—as I fancy it will, Sid—then you must pay that debt, or I'll never forgive you."

"In what way can I ever repay it?"

"By taking your old place at the banker's desk, and showing me that the past is really forgiven."

"I will do that if—ah! what a mighty If this is!"

".Keep hopeful—not nervous, above all the things," said the doctor; "if you fear, it must not be attempted."

With this final warning, the doctor and Maurice withdrew. Maurice left the doctor to whisper confidentially to Mattie.

"Miss Gray, I have brought a skilful oculist to

look at my cousin Sid. He reports not altogether
unfavourably—he gives us hope—Sid will go away
with us to-morrow."

"Go away !"

"Yes, to submit himself for a week or two to
Dr. Bario's treatment; he says that he will chance
the danger, and I think he's right. Keep him
strong and hopeful, Miss Gray—much depends
upon that."

"Yes—yes," gasped Mattie.

She had not recovered her astonishment when
the visitor had left the shop; "hope for Sidney"—
"going away !"—"keep him strong !"—was all this
a dream?

"Mattie," called Sidney from the parlour, and
our heroine rushed in at once and found our hero
walking up and down the room with a freer step
than she had witnessed in him since his blindness.

"Mattie," he said in an agitated voice, "he tells
me that there is a chance of the light coming back
to me—a chance that entails danger, but which is
surely worth the risk. Think of the daylight stream-

ing in upon my darkened senses, and my waking up once more to life!"

"I am so glad!—I am so very glad!" cried Mattie; adding the instant afterwards, "but the—the danger? What is that?"

"A danger of death, or of my going mad, he left it doubtful which—I don't care which—I can risk all for the one chance ahead of me. I will keep strong, praying for the brightness of the new life."

"Yes!" was the mournful response. In that brightness, one figure might at least grow dim—in the darkness he had learned to love her, he said! But he was not thinking of love then, or of her whose love he had sought;—a new hope was bewildering him, and he could not escape it.

"Keep him strong and hopeful," had been the caution given Mattie; there was no need for it. He *was* hopeful—far too hopeful—of the sunshine; he thought nothing of the danger, or of a world a hundred times worse than that of his benighted one—and he was strong in faith. He could talk of nothing else, and Mattie made no effort to distract his mind away from it. It was natural enough that he should forget her for awhile; the time had not come for her to answer him, or to judge him; he had said that his mind was made up, and that she possessed his love—surely they were earnest words enough, to keep her hopeful in her turn?

And if the change in Sidney did result in Sidney's cure, she would rejoice in it with all her heart—as his father would have rejoiced, had he lived and known the troubles of his boy.

The next day, Maurice Hinchford arrived in his father's carriage to take Sidney away. Sidney was equipped for departure, and had been waiting for his cousin the last two hours—agitating his mind with a hundred reasons for the delay.

The carriage at the door, and the evidence of wealth in Sidney's relations, made Mattie's heart sink somewhat—his would be a world so different from hers for ever after this!

Mattie faced Maurice before he entered the parlour. She had been watching for him also that day, and now arrested his progress.

" Mr.. Hinchford, you did me harm once; you were sorry at a later day that it was not in your power to make amends. Will you now?"

"Willingly."

"Let me know when Sidney runs his greatest risk—give me fair warning of it, that his friends may be near him. If there be a risk of death, he must not die without me there. You promise?"

"I promise, Miss Gray."

Mattie had no further request to urge, and he, after avoiding Mr. Gray by a strategic movement, and a hurried "Good day, sir—hope you're well!" entered the parlour with the words—

"Ready, Sid?"

Sidney Hinchford took his friend's arm, Maurice signed to the footman at the door to carry Sidney's portmanteau, and then the two cousins entered the shop—both looking strangely alike, arm-in-arm, and shoulder to shoulder thus.

"One moment, Maurice."

Sidney thought of Mattie at the last; in his own anxiety for self, he did not forget her, as she had feared he would.

"Where's Mattie?"

"Here, Sidney."

He drew her aside—away out of hearing, where
neither Mr. Gray nor his cousin could listen to his
grateful words.

"Mattie, dear," he said, "I know that I shall have
your prayers for my success—you, who have fought
my battles, and been always ready at my side.
Pray for our bright future together; it will come
now. Whatever happens you and I together in
life, my girl, unless, with that month's reflection
that I granted you, comes the want of trust in my
sincerity!"

"Never that, Sidney."

"Good-bye."

He stooped and kissed her, and Mattie shrank
not away from him, though it was the first time in
his life that his lips had touched hers. He was going
away from that house for ever, perhaps; they might
never know each other again; and she loved him
too dearly, and felt too happy in those fleeting moments, to feel abashed at this evidence of his affection.

So they parted, and Ann Packet, who had heard
the story, rushed from the side door to fling a shoe

for luck, after the receding carriage. A maniacal act, that the footman—who had *not* heard the story —was unable to account for, save as a personal insult to himself.

"He had gone out of his spear to a place called Peckham," he said afterwards in the servants' hall, "and had had old boots flung at him by the lower horders!"

CHAPTER II.

MATTIE IS TAKEN INTO CONFIDENCE.

SIDNEY's departure made a difference in the house; it was scarcely home without him now. Mattie and Mr. Gray took their usual places after the day's business was over, and looked somewhat blankly at each other. The father had become attached to Sidney, as well as the daughter; he was nervous as to the result of the mysterious system under which his son, by adoption, had placed himself.

He had no faith in cures effected by men who were not of the true faith—whatever that might mean in Mr. Gray's opinion—he would have liked to see this Dr. Bario himself, and sound him as to his religious convictions. If he were a Roman Catholic, Sidney's chance of success was very small, he thought.

Mattie did not take this narrow view of things; but she was anxious and dispirited. Anxious for Sidney and the result—dispirited at a something else which she could scarcely define. Sidney's last words were ringing in her ears, but there was no comfort in them now; they were meant to encourage, but they only perplexed—all was mystery beyond. She prayed that Sidney would be well and strong again, but she felt that her happiness—her best days—would lie further off when the light came back to him. It might be fancy; the best days might be advancing to her as well as to Sidney Hinchford, but the instinctive feeling of a great change weighed upon her none the less heavily.

She did not feel in suspense about a serious result to Sidney; Sidney would get better, she thought, and the shadow of a darker life for him did not fall heavily athwart her musings.

When those whom we love are away, we are full of wonder concerning them; speculations on their acts in the distance, bridge over the dreary space between us and them. "I wonder

what they are doing now!" and the suggestions that
follow this, wile away a great share of the time
that would seem dull and objectless without them.
You who are loved and are away from us, do
justice to our thoughts of you, and keep worthy
of the fancy pictures wherein ye are so vividly
portrayed !

A week after Sidney's departure, Maurice Hinchford appeared once more in the neighbourhood of
Peckham.   This was in the afternoon, and he had
reached Peckham in the morning, and therefore
wasted a considerable portion of the day.   But
then Mr. Gray had been at home in the morning,
and it had struck Maurice that that gentleman's
excitable temperament would not allow of a long
sojourn in-doors, with no one to preach to but
his daughter.   He would not chance meeting Mr.
Gray yet a while; he would wait and watch.

Mr. Gray really found it dull work that afternoon, and business being slack, he started immediately after his dinner in search of a convert of
whom he had heard in the neighbourhood of his
chapel.   Maurice, who had noted him turn the

corner of the street, uttered a short prayer of thanks, and crossed over to the stationer's shop.

Mattie turned very pale at the first sight of Maurice.

"I am wanted—and, oh dear, my father has just gone out!"

"No, you are not wanted yet a while, Miss Gray. Pray, compose yourself, I bring you very little news."

"Sidney—he is well?"

"Very well—Dr. Bario has not given him notice to prepare for the great experiment yet awhile," said Maurice; "but I thought that you might be anxious about him, Miss Gray, and that any little news might be acceptable."

"You are very kind—yes, any news of Sidney is ever most acceptable."

"Even from such a scamp as I am?" he said, with his eyes twinkling.

"Sidney has forgiven you—that is enough, sir."

"Ah! but yours was a left-handed wrong, and the heaviest share of it might have fallen to your lot."

"But it has not.   Pray don't talk of it again."

"All's well that ends well," said Maurice, taking his seat on the high chair on the shop side of the counter, facing our heroine, "and if it has ended in my doing no harm, and turning out a better fellow myself, why there's not much to regret. And you would not believe to what an extraordinary pitch of excellence I am attaining."

"I shall believe nothing if you jest, sir."

"It was not a jest—I've a way of talking like that."

"It's a very stupid way."

"Is it, though?—well, perhaps you're right enough."

Mattie wondered what he was staying for; was even still a little nervous that he had something more to communicate concerning Sidney. But he continued talking in this new desultory way, and remained on his perch there, observant of customers, the goods they purchased, and the remarks they made, and showing no inclination to depart. He rendered Mattie fidgety after a while, for he was in a fidgety humour himself, and tilted his chair backwards and forwards, and examined everything minutely on the counter, dropping an article or two on the floor, and endeavouring to pick it up with his varnished boots, *à la* Miss Biffin.

" Does this business answer, Miss?" he asked at last.

" It is improving—I think it will answer."

" Rather slow for old Sid, it must have been."

" We did our best to make him happy here, sir; I think that we succeeded."

" My dear Miss Gray, I do not doubt *that*, for an instant!" Maurice hastened to apologize; "more than that, Sidney has told me the same himself. But *was* he happy?"

" Have you any reason to think otherwise?" was Mattie's quick, almost suspicious question.

" Scarcely a reason, perhaps. Still *I* don't think that he was happy."

" I am sorry to hear you say so, Mr. Hinchford."

" He tried to feel as happy as you wished to make him, but I think he failed. Under the circum-

stances, heavily afflicted as he was, you must own
that that was natural."

"I own that."

"But his mind was never at ease—there was
much to perplex it. Now, Miss Gray," leaning
over the counter very earnestly, "let me ask you if
you honestly believe that he has given up every
thought of making Harriet Wesden his wife?"

"Every thought of it, I think he has."

"You and he have been like brother and sister
together, and the truth must have escaped him,"
said Maurice, doubtfully; "or you are less quick-
witted than somehow I have given you credit for.
You would promote his true happiness, Miss Gray,
by every means in your power, I am sure?"

"Yes," answered Mattie.

"Then you and I acting together, might bring
about that match between them yet."

"You and I acting together for that purpose!"
Mattie ejaculated. She clutched the counter with
her nervous fingers, and regarded Maurice Hinchford attentively; she was no longer doubtful of that
man's visit to her; he had come to steal her Sidney

away—to teach her, by his indirect assertions, that it was better to resign her thoughts of happiness rather than mar his cousin's.

"There only requires one fair meeting between them—one candid explanation of what was false, and what was true—to show each to the other in a better light. That is my object in life now—I have done harm to those two—I will do good if I can!"

"You speak as though you were certain of the success of Dr. Bario's remedies."

"I am perfectly certain, Miss Gray! Dr. Bario is certain too—although he speaks of the risk, and of the hundredth chance against him, rather than of the ninety and nine in his favour. That's his way."

"Suppose him successful, and Sidney well again —what are we to do?" asked the curious Mattie.

She was anxious to sift this theory to the bottom —to know upon what facts, or fancies, Maurice Hinchford based his cruel idea. She spoke coolly and sisterly now; no evidence of intense excitement was likely to betray her again that day. On the inner heart had shut, with a clang which vibrated still within her, the iron gates of her inflexible resolve.

"First of all, let me ask 'you a question. You have lived with Miss Wesden—you understand her —you have loved her. You can assure me that there was no doubt of her affection for him being true and fervent?"

"There was no doubt of that."

"I can answer for the present time."

"You can?" said Mattie. She spoke very quickly, but her heart leaped into her throat for an instant, and took away her breath.

"Miss Wesden confessed to me, only a week back, that she loved Sidney Hinchford still."

"Impossible!"

"You doubt my word, Miss Gray. Why should I attempt to deceive you?"

"What possible object could she have in telling you that?"

"I made her an offer of marriage," said Maurice, coolly, "and she rejected me. She did not scruple to confess to me her reasons; she was excited I must own, and, therefore, thrown off her guard."

" What did she say ?"

" That she had never loved me, and that she would have died for Sidney. That it was all my fault—my wickedness—which had parted them."

" A singular confession for her to make," said Mattie, thoughtfully ; " all my life I have been endeavouring to find the truth—the whole truth—and have always failed."

" You were not the confidante that I believed, then ?"

" Harriet Wesden and I loved each other very dearly—in our hearts there is no difference yet. For my sake, were I in danger, she would do much."

" And for her sake—what would you do ?"

" Everything."

" Well spoken," cried Maurice heartily ; "I knew that I was not deceived in you."

" She is unhappy and loves Sidney. Sidney is unhappy and loves her, you think. It is a story of the truth of which we must be certain in the first place."

" Yes, and then ?"

"Then we will do our best—God willing," murmured Mattie.

"I rely upon you, Miss Gray—I am obliged by the evidence of interest in those two old lovers, parted by mistake. Both very unhappy, and both with a chance of being happy together, there is no difficulty in guessing where our duty lies."

"No."

"Think of the gratitude of those two in the days when we have helped to clear the mists away, Miss Gray. The last chapter in the novel; the last scene in the five-act comedy, where the stern parent joins the hands of the happy couple, will be nothing to the glorious ending of *our* story. Boundless gratitude to you, full forgiveness for me—and all going merry as a marriage bell. Miss Gray, I engage your hand for the first dance in the evening—we'll wind up with a ball that day —is it a bargain between us?"

"I make no hasty promises," said Mattie, with a faint smile.

"Well, there will be time to talk of that idea," said Maurice, laughing; "and, talking about time,

how I have been absorbing yours, to be sure! Still
time is well wasted when it is employed for others'
happiness—your father could offer no objection to
that sentiment. You are on my side?"

"On Sidney's, if he think of Harriet Wesden
still."

"If—why, haven't I proved it?—did you not
say that you believed every word?"

"No, I did not. say that. It—it *is* true, perhaps—I shall know better presently. Sir, I will
find out the truth."

¹ "It will be easy for an acute woman to discover
the truth both in Sidney and Harriet; for the
truth—for the better days, we are all waiting.
Good-bye."

"Good-bye, sir; that promise to give me warning of the day which will be life or death to
Sidney—you will not forget?"

"I never forget, Miss Gray. Rely upon me."

Maurice Hinchford departed, full of his hope,
dreaming not of the despair that he had left behind
in the heart of that simple-minded woman. He
had intended all for the best; he had known no-

thing of Sidney's proposal to Mattie; he had relied on Mattie's sisterly affection for the man and woman in whose happiness he was deeply interested. He went on his way rejoicing—proud of the new volunteer he had enlisted in his cause, and sanguine as to a result which should bring peace to every one.

Mattie sat behind the counter in her old position after Maurice Hinchford had left her—rigid and motionless. This was the turning-point of her life —the ordeal under which she would harden or utterly give way. A customer entering the shop waited and stared and wondered at the silent figure which faced him and took no heed of his presence —at her who was finally roused to every-day life by his direct appeal to her. Mattie served him, then dropped into her chair again, and the old stony look settled once more upon her face.

Fate was before her, and she rebelled against it; the whole truth—hard and cruel—she could not believe in. "It's not true!" her white lips murmured; "it's false, as he is! He has heard from Sidney all that Sidney purposes, and is alarmed

for the honour of his family. I see it all now—a
plot against me!" But "was it true?" sounded in
her ears like a far-off echo, from which she could
not escape.

It was a desperate struggle, and she was fighting
that silent intense battle still when her father
returned. Hours ago she had prayed that he
might come back soon, and end that weary watch
there—suffer her to escape to her own room, and
lock the door upon that world upon which the
mists were stealing. But when he returned, she
did not go away from him; a horror of being
alone and giving way like a child kept her at her
post there, answering, and inwardly defying, all
suspicious questions.

"You're very white, Mattie? Has anything happened?" asked her father.

"Sidney's cousin has been here. Sidney is well
and hopeful."

"Good hearing!—he will be back in the midst
of us before we know where we are. Mattie, I'm
sure you have a headache?"

"A little one—nothing to complain about."

" Why don't you go for a walk?—it's not very late. What a time it is since you have seen Mr. Wesden !"

"I will go there."

Mattie sprang to her feet.

" Yes, I *will* go—at once."

Mattie ran upstairs, quickly dressed herself, gave one frightened glance at her own face in the dressing-glass, and then hurried downstairs away from the silence wherein she could not trust herself.

" I am going now," she said, and hurried away.

Mr. Gray was disturbed by Mattie's eagerness to depart, but explained it by the rules he considered most natural.

" She is unsettled by Sid's absence—by the danger he is in. Well, there's nothing remarkable in that."

He took his work into the shop and devoted himself to it, in the leisure that his customers—few and far between after nightfall—afforded him. When the shutters were up before the windows, and the gas turned low, he stood at the door waiting for Mattie, who was late, and speculating as to the advisability of proceeding in search of her.

Mattie came swiftly towards him whilst he watched. She had been trying to outwalk her thoughts, and failed—the odds were against her.

"Ah! that is you, Mattie!—how are they?"

"Well. I did not see Miss Wesden. She was not at home."

"All the time with that old man?" he said, with a little of his past weakness developing itself.

"We have been speaking of old times—and Harriet. Oh! dear! I am very tired. May I go up to my room at once?"

"If you will—but supper is ready, Mattie."

"Not any for me. Good night."

Mattie thought that she had made good her escape, but she was mistaken; on the stairs Ann Packet had been waiting to waylay her, and to talk of the little events of that day—any talk whatever, so that she saw Mattie for a while, after the day's labour was ended. Mattie was considerate even in her distress; she stood on the stairs listening to Ann's rambling accounts of minor things, waiting for the end of the narrative, and only expressing her weariness by a little quivering sigh, now and then.

After the story there was Ann Packet to hold the candle closer to her face, and see a change in Mattie also. Mattie had feared this—knowing Ann's vigilance—but there was the old plea of a headache to urge, and all the old receipts of which Ann Packet had ever heard for the headache to listen to. Ann Packet knew an old woman of her workhouse days who had had "drefful headaches," and this was how she cured hers—and off went Ann Packet into more rambling incoherencies.

All things have an end; Mattie was free at last. At last the door locked, and the room she had longed for, feared, and longed for again, engulphing her. . Mattie took off her bonnet, opened noiselessly the window for the air which she felt she needed, and then dropped into a chair, and looked out at the dark sky, and the bright stars that were shimmering up there, where all seemed peace !

The battle was not over, and Mattie was unconvinced still.

"Is it true?" she asked again ; " is it ALL true !"

CHAPTER III.

HALF THE TRUTH.

MATTIE, as we are already aware, had found Mr. Wesden the sole occupant of that house in Camberwell, whither the stationer had retired from the stirring business of life. He was alone, dull and dispirited; Harriet had gone to a thanksgiving festival at her favourite church, and her father, whom night-air affected now, was left to read his newspaper, or to think of old times, as his inclination might suggest.

Harriet always offered to remain at home to keep her father company, but old Wesden was not a selfish man; he offered no objection to her departure; it would do her good, and be a change for her. It had long ago suggested itself to him that there was no-

thing like change to keep Harriet well and all unpleasant thoughts away from her; and if it were
only the mild excitement of religious change, it
was better than brooding at home over events
which had passed and left marks of their ravages.

Mr. Wesden brightened up at Mattie's visit;
he had put away his pipe, and was sitting with
his feet on the fender and his hands on his knees,
thinking of his daughter and of the chance she
had lost in not marrying Maurice Hinchford, when
Mattie intruded on his reverie.

The old friends—friends who had quarrelled
and made it up, and become the best of friends
again—sat down together and talked of the past,
of what a business that was in Suffolk Street once,
slow, and sure, and money-getting. Mr. Wesden
was inclined to talk more in his old age, Mattie
fancied, and when he drifted to the usual subject
with which all topics invariably ended—his daughter
—Mattie did not stop him.

She had come to find out the truth, if possible
—to make sure! Next to Sidney Hinchford, stood
Harriet Wesden in her regard; she remembered

all that Harriet had been to her, all that impulsiveness of action combined with steadiness of
love which had won Mattie towards her in the early
days, and was not likely to turn her from her
then.

But the truth had been hard to arrive at; Mr.
Wesden spoke of Harriet's new pursuits, of her
indignation at Maurice Hinchford's offer; he could
tell her little more than Maurice Hinchford had
done, save that there were times when his daughter
seemed very dull and thoughtful.

"P'raps it's the church, Mattie," he had said;
"I wish you'd come more often and talk to her,
like—like you used."

" She does not think that I have neglected her
—forgotten her?"

"Oh! no."

" When I meet her here, she seems very different
to me—almost cold at times," said Mattie.

" Only her way, Mattie," explained the father,
" she's very different to all, now. She was more
like herself after Mr. Hinchford called—Lor'! that
roused her for a day or two beautifully. It was

quite a treat to see her out of temper all the next day—flouting like !"

Mattie waited till half-past eight, and then took her leave, thinking that she would go home by the church-way and meet Harriet. But Harriet had gone round by the main thoroughfare, having a call to make, and so the old companions missed each other.

Mattie scarcely knew what she should have said to Harriet on meeting her, save the usual common-place remarks; she fancied that she might have told her story of Sidney's proposal, and watched the effect—might have looked her sternly in the face, and asked if it were all true that Maurice Hinchford had asserted. It depended upon circum-stances what she would have confessed or asserted; after all, did it matter what were Harriet Wesden's feelings, if Sidney had ceased to love Harriet and turned to Mattie Gray ?

But Sidney was blind *then*, and his heart, ever full of gratitude, had deceived him. Perhaps he *had* read her secret by some means, and taken pity on her. *Pity !*—and she had told him that she scorned it! Well, true or false, right or wrong, she must wait a few days longer—for better, for worse, there was no keeping that truth back, unless it died with Sidney.

Mattie made the best of it, as usual. Hers was a mind of uncommon strength, although her slight figure and gentle face suggested to an observer the very reverse of a "strong-minded woman." The next day, she was the Mattie that deceived even her father, who had been alarmed at her yester-night. She had got over her headache, she said; she could talk of business-matters, and of going to the warehouse for fresh stock, of the customers on "the books," and of the customers—a few of them by the laws of business—who were never likely to get off them. In the morning, too, came an immense order, that staggered Mr. Gray—an order for stationery, pens, ink, and paper, &c., from Hinchford and Son, bankers.

"They've given their relation a turn—I don't think Sid would like it much," said Mr. Gray.

Mattie affected an interest in these new customers, and Mr. Gray, who admired large orders, though he was not a worldly man, trotted about the shop and rubbed his hands. The first customer who entered, and told him that it was a fine day, was assured that " Yes it was. A fine order, a very fine order indeed !"

Orders taken, delivered, and goods paid for; time making inroads into the new week; people be-gining to talk of coming spring, and of the cold weather breaking up for good; Mattie waiting for the summons to Sidney Hinchford's side, and wondering why Dr. Bario was so long; the hour in which to answer Sidney approaching, and she still unresolved as to what was best and just—for others, as well as for herself !

The message came at last—by special messenger, and private cab ; a dashing Hansom, with the Hinchford crest on the panel, drawn by a thorough-bred mare, which brought out all the horse-fanciers from the livery-stables at the corner to look at and admire.

Mattie opened Maurice Hinchford's hastily written note.

"Dear Miss Gray," it ran, "we have resolved upon the operation to-day. Sidney is prepared—calm and hopeful of the result. I never knew a fellow with so little fear· in him. Bring Miss Wesden if you think fit.

"Yours very truly,

"MAURICE HINCHFORD."

Bring Miss Wesden! Mattie had never thought of that, and for the first time the woman's natural jealousy seized her. Take her rival to his side, and let *her* comfort him, and she standing aloof and unacknowledged!—why should she do that? Thrust upon Sidney Hinchford's thoughts, at such a time, the old love ; let him *see*, perhaps, Harriet Wesden's beauty and her own plain face side by side, the very instant that he stepped back, as it were, to. his old self !

Then came better thoughts—thoughts more true to this high-minded stray of ours. It was light, or madness, or death ; if it were a failure, and he should die, swiftly and suddenly—if till the last he had deceived her, and his true nature were

to assert itself, and he express a wish—one last
yearning wish to see Harriet Wesden—what could
she say?—in the future how that reproach of not
having done her best would crush her with remorse !

She was in the cab; she had made up her mind ;
there was to be no longer any hesitation.

" Drive to Myer's Street, Camberwell."

The thorough-bred mare stepped out and cleared
the roadway; the shop and the little excited man
at its door were in the background, and Mattie was
being whirled along to Mr. Wesden's house. In a
very little while, Mattie was driven to the old
friend's.   Mr. Wesden was gardening in his
fore-court, or attempting something of the kind,
with a little rake he had bought at a toy-shop; he
dropped his rake, and stared over the private cab
and its occupant at the upstair's windows of the
opposite residence.

" Mattie," he said, when she was at the gate,
and had opened it and entered before he had recovered his astonishment, " what's the matter?
Who's cab is that?—the stationery business won't
stand cabs, yet awhile, I know."

"Where is Harriet?—not out again?"

"No, in the parlour—this way."

Mattie and Mr. Wesden entered the house. Harriet was in the front parlour—the best room, which had been Mrs. Wesden's pride, and a dream of the old lady's in business days, —working busily away at a pair of crimson slippers, with large black crosses on the instep— High Church slippers, every inch of them. Not slippers for a simpering curate to receive anonymously, as a mark of esteem from a fair unknown— Harriet was above that; but good colossal slippers, for the gouty feet of her pastor and master, who could not wear tight boots in the house, and had even been known to preach in something easy.

Harriet, who had noted the arrival, was ready to receive Mattie. She ran to her and kissed her. Harriet's first impulse was a kind and loving one whenever she met Mattie first; only as the interview lengthened, did her doubts—if they could be called doubts—step in and range themselves formally beside her, and render her almost reserved. The kiss with which they parted, always savoured

more of the new Harriet, than of the bright-faced
beauty whom Sidney had *once* loved, Mattie thought.

"Harriet, I want you to come with me, if you
will," said Mattie.

"I am rather busy just now, Mattie," said Harriet; "where do you wish to take me?"

"To see Sidney Hinchford," was the calm reply.

"To see *whom!*" ejaculated Harriet.

Before Mattie could explain, Harriet added—

"What object can you have in taking me to
him?—in coming in this strange hurried manner
for me?   Has *he* sent you?"

"No."

"He has no wish that I should be near him, I
am sure.   This is eccentric and foolish—what do
you mean by it?"

Harriet's haughty gesture would have done more
credit to royal blood than to old Wesden's.

Mattie caught her by the wrist, so that Harriet
should not escape her, or hide any sign of emo-
tion which she might wish to conceal when all was
known.

"You must come!   There is no excuse.   In a

few hours Sidney Hinchford may be dead!"

Did the change upon that face tell all, or was it the natural result of such news as Mattie had hissed forth?

"Dead!—dead did you say?" asked Harriet, hastily.

"I did not tell your father a few nights ago that Sidney had left us—I reserved the news for you, and then missed you going home. He is in the hands of clever and scientific men, who hope to cure him of his blindness."

"Yes—go on."

"But there is a chance of failure, which Sidney risks, and thinks, perhaps, too lightly of. That failure will not subject him to his old estate, but drive him mad, or kill him."

"And you have let him risk his life—you!"

Away went the ecclesiastical slippers to the other end of the room; some wool got entangled in her hands, and she snapped it impatiently in two in preference to unwinding it; she turned to Mattie, full of reproach, fear, and indignation. Yes, the love was living still! Mattie might have known long ago that it had never died away, and that to keep it in subjection had been the task which Harriet had set herself, and failed in.

"They will murder him!—you have let them take him away to work their dangerous experiments upon, and you will have to answer for this!"

"Sidney was resolved—his cousin wished it—I had no power to stop it."

"Mattie, he loves you. He would have done as you wished."

"Who says he loves me?" asked Mattie. "I have never uttered a word to give you that belief, Harriet—have I?"

"No—but——"

"I don't own it now—I say nothing, but ask you to come with me. If I loved him, or mistrusted you, should I be here?"

"What am I to do?" asked the bewildered Harriet. "Oh! tell me, what can I do?"

"Maurice Hinchford thinks it possible—I think it possible—that Sidney may wish to speak to you before or afterwards. We may retire and see him not, or we may face him. If it should end as we all pray not, and hope not, you, at least, must not be away!"

"No, no!—I would not be away from him for all the world," cried Harriet. "I will go with you at once."

She darted out of the room, and Mr. Wesden seemed to take her place as if by magic before Mattie.

"What's it all mean, my girl?"

Mattie had to struggle with many conflicting emotions, and sober down sufficiently to relate the nature of her visit. Before she had half finished her statement, Harriet was with them again.

"Let us go at once, Mattie!—father will hear all when I return."

She almost dragged Mattie from the room; they were both in the cab, and rattling away from Camberwell, before Mr. Wesden fully comprehended that they had left him.

"Mattie, it is kind of you to think of me at this time," said Harriet. "You have read me more

Q 2

truly than I have read myself.   I am a wicked and
unjust woman."

"No—that's not true."

"I have had wicked thoughts of you—you that
I have known so long, and should have estimated
so truly, knowing what you have ever been to me.
But, oh! Mattie, I have been so wretched and unhappy, that you *will* forgive me?"

"Don't say any more, please."

Harriet looked askance at the pale face beside
her—the eyes were half closed, and the thin lips
compressed.

" Do you feel ill?"

" No—the excitement of all this may have been
a little too much for me—we will not talk of ourselves just now.   Time enough for your confession,
and for mine, when we return."

"How shall we return?—with what hopes or
fears of him?   What made his cousin and you
think of me being near him?   Did *he* wish it?"

"I don't know."

" Has *he* thought of me all this while?—loved
me despite all?   Oh! if that were true, Mattie."

"If it were true, Harriet—what a difference!"

"And now perhaps to die, and I never to know his real thoughts of me. Well, I should die too—I'm sure of that now!"

"Harriet, you can trust me again?"

"Yes, with all my heart."

"Patience, then—we *will* say no more until we are sure that the truth faces us."

They were silent for the remainder of the way; people who passed on the footpath, and glanced towards the occupants of that private cab, wondered at the two pale, grave-faced women sitting side by side therein.

CHAPTER IV.

ALL THE TRUTH.

THE house wherein Sidney was waiting for the best or worst, was situated in Bayswater. A house that had been taken at Maurice's expense, and by Dr. Bario's suggestion. The Italian doctor was a man with a love of effect—one of those stagey beings whom we meet occasionally in England, and more often on the Continent. He was fond of mystery; it enhanced the surprise, and gained him popularity. He was a clever man, but he was also a vain one.

His style of practice he kept to himself; whether his cures were effected by the common methods of treatment, or by methods of his own, were hard to arrive at; he bound his patients and his patients' friends to secrecy; some of his English medical

contemporaries called him a quack, others a mad-
man—a few, just a few, to leaven the mass, thought
that there *was* something in him. Abroad he
was at the top of the tree and sought after—matter-
of-fact England not being able to make him
out, eyed him suspiciously.

Mattie and Harriet were ushered into a well-
furnished room on the first floor, where Maurice
Hinchford awaited them. He went towards them
at once, and shook hands with them—even with
Harriet Wesden, who had faced him with such
stern words during their last interview. There was
a common cause that bound all three together, and
the past was forgotten.

" We are in time?" asked Mattie.

" Plenty of time, thank you."

" Where is Sidney ?"

" In the room beyond there, where the curtain
hangs before the door."

" Have you told him that *we* are here?" asked
Mattie.

" Yes, he is very anxious to speak with you
both before he is left in Dr. Bario's hands."

"You are hopeful of good results?" asked Harriet.

"Yes—very hopeful—are not you?" he asked curiously.

"No—I fear the worst."

"You have not considered the matter, Miss Wesden—this has come upon you with the shock of a surprise, and hence the feeling that distresses you. But I say he shall get better—we have all determined to make an extraordinary case of him."

"Hush, sir!—he is in God's hands, not yours," said Harriet.

"I beg pardon—of course."

Maurice withdrew, a little downcast at Harriet's reproof; he had assumed an over-cheerful air to set them at their ease, and they had not understood him. They fancied that he was not anxious, when he felt all a brother's suspense. He had been with Sidney day and night; he had studied Sid's wishes, sought to keep him cheerful, read to him, had wound himself into Sid's heart, and by the act enlarged his own and purified it. The cousins understood each other; all the past had been atoned for now; there was no element of bitterness in the forgiveness which Maurice had sought and Sidney granted.

Maurice was called away, and presently returned with the Italian doctor, to whom he introduced Miss Wesden.

"What is there to fear, sir?" was Harriet's first question.

She had heard all from Mattie, but was not satisfied until all had been told her again from the doctor's lips. He still spoke of the chances for and against success.

Presently, and before he had concluded, Mr. Geoffry Hinchford was ushered into the room and introduced to the ladies there.

After a bow of the old-fashioned school, he said—

"This young lady," indicating Mattie, "I have had the pleasure of seeing before. Some years ago, when she thought I had a design to rob a shop in Suffolk Street. Am I right, Miss Gray?"

He spoke in jest, but Mattie responded gravely enough. It was no time for jesting, and she

thought that Mr Geoffry Hinchford's remarks were
strangely *mal-ápropos*. His manner changed, when
he faced Doctor Bario in his turn.

" You must cure this patient, sir, and name your
own terms.   My son and I will chance your breaking the bank."

" You are good—very," said the pleased doctor,
" and I am much obliged."

" We shall have him at his old post, I hope,
ladies," said he, veering round to the fair sex again.
" A banking-house is his proper sphere—he will
rise to greatness with a fair chance. I do not
know any man who deserves greatness better—a
true man of business—what a contrast to his poor
father !"

Maurice had withdrawn, and now returned
again.

" He is ready to see the ladies now; keep him
up, please, and speak cheerfully of the future—
that's right, doctor, I believe ?"

" Quite right."

" One at a time. Mattie, he will see you first,
he says."

Mattie's heart leaped anew at this; she passed beneath the curtain which Maurice Hinchford held above her head, and went through the door to a large room where Sidney was awaiting her. The sun was shining through the windows upon him —a pale, calm figure, sitting there.

"Mattie," he said.

"Yes—I have come."

The door opened again, and Doctor Bario entered, taking up a position where he could watch his patient's face. There must be nothing calculated to excite his patient now.

Sidney shook hands with Mattie, saying—

"It has come at last—and we shall know the worst or the best in a few minutes."

"You are not nervous of the result?—your pulse beats calmly, Sidney."

"I have steeled my nerves to it—I shall not shrink, and I am hopeful."

"Miss Wesden is here."

"You fetched her hither, Maurice tells me," he answered. "You are not a jealous woman, Mattie."

"Have I a right to be jealous yet, before my mind is made up?" she answered, lightly.

"The month draws on apace—I am looking forward to the future."

"Time," said Doctor Bario, and Mattie withdrew, after a silent pressure of hands, given and returned. Mattie went towards the doctor instead of the door.

"These interviews must tend to excite him—his pulse is less regular than it was, sir."

"I am sorry for it," said Bario, coolly, "but he will have his way—he is one man impetuous in that. He thinks it is better, in *case of anything!*"

Mattie backed from him in horror; did Sid. fear the result of the experiment himself now? Harriet was waiting anxiously for her return.

"Be careful," whispered Mattie, as she passed in, and Mattie followed her with her wistful eyes. They were a long while together, she thought; longer than was necessary, or Doctor Bario should have allowed. What had Harriet Wesden to say to him?—what would she say in moments like those?

The curtain was drawn back, and Harriet, with flushed checks, and tearful eyes, came rapidly towards Mattie.

"What have you said to him?" asked Mattie, almost fiercely.

"What I would have said to him had he been dying—as he will die!—oh! as he will die, I am sure of it."

"I pray God not," ejaculated Mattie.

"I asked him if he had forgiven me—if he would believe that when he gave me up I loved him with my whole heart, and looked for no happiness without him."

"You told him that!—you dared to tell him that at such a time!"

"I could not have told him at any other, and he was about to be sacrificed by his own will and, these mad relations, who have persuaded him to this! He will die, I am sure of it!"

"Don't say it again—I must hope, Harriet, and you drive me mad by this excitability. What have you done?"

"Strengthened his courage—been rewarded by

the 'God bless you, Harriet!' which escaped him."

" Did he say no more ?"

" Nothing but 'Too late!' In his heart he must
feel that he will *die*, or he would not have said
that. Oh! those awful words, which will ring in
our ears and be our torment when this is over.
Mattie, I must stop it !"

Mattie held the excited girl in her own strong
arms, and backed her to a greater distance from the
door of the room where Sidney was ; at the same
moment the banker returned from his fugitive interview with his nephew, and stood at the window
taking snuff by wholesale. A confusion seemed to
suddenly pervade the scene; an assistant, then
another entered, and passed into Sidney's room ; a
third assistant ushered across the room wherein
they waited, a physician, with whom Mr. Geoffry Hinchford shook hands, and took snuff for
an instant. Maurice looked through the curtain
for an instant, held up his hand, and then withdrew again. The instant afterwards the door was
locked on the inner side, and a silence as of death
settled upon the three watchers without.

All was still; the thick walls and the closed doors deadened every sound. Once and only once Dr. Bario's voice giving some orders startled the banker and the two girls cowering at the extremity of the room.

"How still!" whispered Harriet at last, and Mattie bade her be silent. Mattie was listening with strained ears for sounds from within, and the fear that had beset Harriet settled at last upon herself and unnerved her. How long would it be now, each thought and wondered—minutes, hours, or what?

"This waiting is very awful," said Mr. Geoffry Hinchford, suddenly, and Mattie bade him hush also, in an angry tone that made him jump again.

Suddenly the door was unlocked, and the three started up with clenched hands and suspended breath. Two of the assistants came forth hurriedly, and went out of the room. To the eager questions that were put to them they answered something in Italian, and balked the longing of their questioners. Then Maurice appeared, and cried,

" Success!—success! A statue in gold for Dr. Bario! The——"

" Hinchford," called the doctor from within, "come back—he calls you."

" No, not me," said Maurice, whose ears caught the English accent more perfectly, "*he calls Harriet*—may she come?"

" Yes, for an instant—quick!"

Harriet darted across the room with a suppressed cry; the old fear had seized her again.

" He is dying!—I knew it!"

"No, no, he will live for you!" cried Mattie, wringing her hands together; " go to him!"

Harriet passed into the room, and recoiled for an instant at the utter darkness and blackness of the place she had left so light. Maurice put his hands upon her wrist, and drew her forwards. Dr. Bario's voice arrested him.

" He has fainted—take her out again. He must speak to no one any more to-day."

" But he will die!—oh! sir, will he not die?" cried Harriet.

"He will live; he will be as well in three weeks as ever—please withdraw."

Harriet and Maurice Hinchford came back together.

"There is no use in waiting," Maurice said; "the result is as successful as I anticipated. Let me recommend you to return home at once, Miss Wesden. Miss Gray will accompany you, I am sure."

"Mattie, will you come with me?" asked Harriet, faintly.

Mattie moved like an automaton towards her, and the two went out together arm-in-arm, down the broad stair-case to the hall, from the hall to the street, where Maurice's cab still waited for them.

"I am faint and ill, Mattie," said Harriet, sinking back.

"Will you rest awhile?"

"No—let us get home at once. How coldly and quietly you take this news, Mattie!" she said, looking intently at her; "ah! if you had only loved him like me all your life!"

R

" If I had !" murmured Mattie, "*this* would have broken my heart !"

" Hearts don't break with joy, Mattie, or I should not see another morning."

"No.   You are right—not with joy !"

CHAPTER V.

STRUGGLING.

HAD Harriet Wesden been less disturbed by all
the trials of that day, she might have wondered
more at Mattie's manner, and have guessed more
shrewdly at the truth. But she had suspected un-
justly; and feeling now that Sidney loved her,
and had always loved her, there were dissipated for
ever all bitter memories. It was Mattie's turn to
change, but Harriet did not notice it at that time;
Mattie had become distant, grave; in the first
shock of the real truth—though Mattie had seen it
advancing, and thought herself prepared to meet it
—it was impossible to smile and feel content.
Harriet was anxious that the old friend should stay
with her at Camberwell for awhile, but Mattie was
firm in her refusal.

" I must get home—I am very weary!" she murmured.

So they had parted, and Mattie had returned home to offer the great news concerning Sidney, and then escape to her room and be seen no more that night. What happened on that night—what resolves, what struggles, we need not dwell on here ; she was one who had been injured—the best of women come in for the greatest injuries at times—and it was not a night's thought or struggle which could set her right. She was a heroine, but she was a woman—and women brood on matters which affect the heart for a long, long time after we have been deceived by their looks.

Mattie did not blame Sidney; she saw how far he had been led to deceive himself, and how far pity and gratitude had betrayed him; she knew that he considered himself bound to her still, and that only her word could release him from his. She felt that he was miserable like herself, and she fretted impatiently for the day when she could let him go free to his sphere, and to the only woman whom he had loved.

But the change had not been good for her; she was not resigned yet; her heart was in rebellion. Life before her seemed a dreary vista—a blankness on which no light could shine; ever in the world ahead, she traced her figure plodding onwards without a motive in life, or a hope that had not been lost in it—from first to last, only in various disguises, and on different roads, ever the Stray!

Was she better off now than in the old, old days when she walked the London streets bare-footed, and sang or begged for bread—even stole for it once or twice? No one had loved her then, or taken heed of her; a few had pitied her at that time as they might pity her in this, if she were weak enough to tell her story to them. Her father would pity her, but did he love her, she thought gloomily? She was not inclined to do him justice in that dark estate of hers; he had never wholly understood her; she had become a necessity to his existence, and he was grateful for it, as Sidney had been grateful—nothing more! Yes, she stood alone—for the love and generous hearts around her womanhood, she might be on a mountain top, with the cold, unsympathetic winds freezing her as she lingered there. Almost with regret she looked back at the past, and wondered if it had been well to save her from the dangers that surrounded her; she might have fought against them, and grown up more ignorant perhaps, but more loved. In a different sphere she would have made different friends, and known nothing of this *genteel* life, where there had been no happiness, and much trouble and remorse!

Hence, by noting Mattie's thoughts, we arrive at the conclusion that this was Mattie's darkest hour; that a change had befallen her which time might remedy, or might harden within her to a wrong—it depended upon the forces brought to bear upon her, and her own heart's strength.

She had heard nothing of Sidney since the experiment in a direct manner. Maurice had met her father in the streets, and informed him that all was progressing well, and Sidney was gaining ground rapidly—that had been " information enough for the Grays," Mattie thought, a little bitterly; there was no occasion for further visits to out-of-the-way districts, now the banker's son could exult over the result of his scheming! From Harriet no news had reached her, and Mattie had not sallied forth in search of her. The day on which Mattie was to have made up her mind and answered Sidney came and went without anyone taking heed of it. When would the sign come that he remembered her?— what would he do and say when he was well again? —what would he think of *her?*

Mr. Gray did not observe any particular change in his daughter; she was graver and more thoughtful, but he attributed that to her concern for Sidney's recovery. Once he was about to speak of Sidney's proposal to Mattie, and was asked, almost imploringly, to say no more; but he was not alarmed. Mattie was nervous still, and had not recovered the shock yet. She was his dutiful daughter whom he loved, and though her grave face did not become her years, still it was the face of a girl who took things studiously and reverently, and he was proud of it. Serious people suited Mr. Gray; his daugh-

ter was becoming every day more worthy of him,
thank God!

Still there was one watcher on whom Mattie had
not reckoned—a watcher who knew all the story,
and guessed more than Mattie could have wished—
to whom every change in Mattie was a thing of
moment, which affected her.   This humble agent,
who had watched thus, since the time Mattie was a
child, had some inkling of the truth—hearts that
have but one idol are sensitive enough.   Through
the stolidity, the inflexibility of Mattie, Ann Packet
read the despair, and charged it with her honest force.

One night, when Mattie thought that the house
was quiet for good—meaning by that, that her
father and Ann Packet were in their rooms, and
asleep—she was sitting by her little toilet-table,
dwelling upon a hundred associations, that all verged
to one common centre, when a tapping on the
panels of her door startled her.

"Who's there?" she asked; "is that you, Ann?"

"Yes—let me in."

She demanded it as a right, rather than as a
favour, but Mattie admitted her without opposition.

Ann Packet entered with her cap awry—hanging in fact, by strange filaments, to her back comb— and she placed herself in front of Mattie, with her arms akimbo, quite defiantly.

" Now, what's the matter with *you* ?"

" Have I complained ?—is there likely to be any- thing the matter, Ann ?"

" Yes, there is. And you'll just tell me, please, what is it !"

" Ann, you forget yourself."

" No, it's you who is forgetting yourself, and me, and all you had a liking and a love for wunst. It's you as has altered so dreffully, that I can only think of one thing to make you different."

" Don't tell me !—don't tell me !" Mattie en- treated.

Ann Packet took no heed.

" It's *him !*" she whispered.

Mattie did not answer ; she went back to her seat by the toilet-table, and turned her head away from the one faithful to her, to the last. She was vexed that she had not kept her secret closer, and deceived them *all !*

" It's no good telling me it ain't him, Mattie—cos it is !" Ann Packet said, after following Mattie to the table, and taking another chair facing her; " there's nothing else—there can't be nothing else, girl.   Well, I wouldn't grieve because his sight's come back—that's not right !"

" Do you think I grieve for that ?" cried Mattie, fired into defence; " oh ! Ann, how can you ever think so badly of me !"

" Then you're afraid that he won't like you any more ?"

" How do you know he ever liked me, or said he did ?"

" I—I guessed as much."

Ann Packet, we know, possessed a secret as well as Mattie.

" You guessed wrongly."

" I guessed what you did, Mattie—there !"

" I am not always in the right, Ann," was the hard answer; " I am a foolish woman, ever ready to drop into the snare of a few fine words !"

Ann scarcely understood her; but she went on resolutely—

" You think he's tired of you—that it won't come right now. Why not ?"

" Nothing can come right out of nothing," said Mattie, passionately, and not too clearly ; " I can't be worried like this, Ann. I have nothing to tell you ; I am what I have always been. If there be a difference, it is only that I am getting older, and more world-worn. Won't you believe me ?"

" No, I won't. I think I know you well enough by this time, and aren't to be *done* by any reason short of what's a true un. Oh ! Mattie gal, you're not happy ; you, who have done so much for happiness to tother people—and this shan't be, if I can help it ! You and Mr. Hinchford must get married ; and if there's been a quarrel, *that'll* mend it."

" Mr. Hinchford and I will never marry, Ann."

" You mean it ?"

" Yes."

" I don't see why," said Ann, reflectively.

" Mr. Hinchford will marry Harriet Wesden— they are old lovers, and true ones." .

Ann Packet looked fixedly for awhile at Mattie, and then burst forth :

"Let him! Pr'aps he's fitter for her than you, if he's weak-minded and babyish, and can't tell what's best for him. Let him pack up his traps and go—you can do without him." Ann Packet, carried away by the feelings of the moment, went on, in a higher key. "You're too good for him, and the likes of him, and ain't agoing begging because a pink-faced gal is set afore ye. You're young yet. You've people to love you, and take care on you—you shan't be lonely, and you shall get over all your disappintments and be as happy as the day is long. It isn't for you, Mattie, to fret yourself to death because a little trouble's come, and you can't shake it off yet—you'll show 'em that you've never been a fretting, and that you've got a consolation yet, that their goings on can't take away!"

"Well, Ann, where would be your consolation?" asked Mattie.

"Where you taught me to find it, big words and all—where you will never lose it, Mattie, good as you've growed."

There was something touching in the manner

with which Ann Packet snatched from the toilet-
table the little Bible that always had a place there,
and laid it suddenly in Mattie's lap. Mattie
shivered, even cowered somewhat at the demonstra-
tion; it had been unexpected as that interview,
and for the first time in her life Ann Packet took
the vantage ground, and Mattie looked up to *her*.

"When you turned good, Mattie," said Ann,
"you turned to *that*—you read it to me, and tried
to make me read it, telling me that there was comfort to be found there for my loneliness. *I* found
it—so will you, child. *You* can't miss what you
found me!"

"It does not follow," murmured Mattie.

"Yes it does," said Ann, who would not abate
one jot of her assertions; "with *you*, who ain't like
tother people, and who never was. You liked tother
people better than yourself, and so got posed upon
—but you're all the better for it—lor bless you!—
you'll see that in *there*. And, Mattie, there's your
father and me, still—we shan't drop away from
you. The likes of me," she added, after a little

more reflection, " isn't much to brag on, but you'll find me allus true—that's something."

" Everything !"

" You ain't like me, with no one to look to—with no one but you in all the world that would do me a good turn if I wished it ever so. With you there isn't one but'd go anywhere to help you, knowing what a contented soul you are. And when it comes to you, allus so cheerful, getting mopish—you, who finds somethin' good in things that others fret at, and makes us warm and comfurble instead o' shivering with fright—why, it's sixes and sevens all a topsy turvy anyhow, and no one to look up to nowhere !"

" I must come back to my old self, if I have wandered from it so much that your honest heart is touched by the change, Ann," said Mattie. " Perhaps I have been gloomy without a cause— perhaps you are right and I am wrong—though I don't confess to all your implications, mind—and from you I can bear to hear my lesson better than from others at this time. Ann, I'm not going to break my heart."

" God bless you ! I knew that."

" I'm going to be just my old self again—nothing more. Not quite that, suddenly, but finding my way back, as it were. There, you'll leave me now—to think."

" Only to think ?" said Ann, with a wistful look at the holy volume in her lap ; " it's too much thinking that has done this harm."

" To think what is best, Ann," said Mattie, rising, " and, failing that, to pray for it ; there, leave me now. Don't fear for me ever again."

" And I haven't done wrong in talking of all this—you were angry when I first comed in, Mattie?"

" I am glad that you came now—I must have been aging very rapidly to have alarmed one who always had such trust in me. It's all over now!"

When Ann Packet had withdrawn, Mattie clasped her hands together and cried again, " It is all over!" as though for ever some hope had been dismissed rather than some fear. Hopes and fears had perhaps gone down the stream of time together, and it was impossible to arrest the sighs for the fair blossoms which had been once. But she was stronger from that day; Mattie was not likely to harden, and it had only needed one warm-hearted counsellor to turn her from the wrong path she was pursuing. The right counsellor had come —a humble messenger, but a true one; one to whom Mattie could listen without shame.

"I was never fit for him—in his new estate, I might have brought him shame rather than happiness—and it was his happiness I tried for, not my own!"

She sank down on her knees and prayed as honest Ann had wished. But she did not pray for the best to happen as she had promised. She knew what was best for her and others—so far as it is possible to know that—and she asked for strength to do her best.

CHAPTER VI.

SIGNS OF CHANGE.

MR. GRAY, though he had not remarked any change that was prejudicial to his daughter Mattie, was quick enough to detect the new difference in her manner. He knew then that she had not been "her old self," as Ann Packet had termed it, by the old manner which was now substituted. She was more gentle, less distracted, kinder in her way altogether, more thoughtful of what his requirements consisted, and which was the best way to expedite them. If she smiled with an effort still, *that* he did not remark; he felt the benefit of the change and was content with it; he knew no reason why there should be any effort in her looks.

He expected to hear all on the first day that

Mattie had received good news of Sidney Hinchford; that he was quite well perhaps, and coming
back to his old home for a while—coming back to
settle *that* engagement. He did not suggest the
name however; he waited for suggestions. Mattie
had shown that she was tenacious on that question
of engagement, and far from disposed to state her
ultimate intentions. He could afford to wait,
knowing that all was well!

In the evening his forbearance was rewarded
by Mattie speaking of Sidney. She knew that to
hold that name for ever in the background was
unnatural. She was anxious to keep it a well
known name, and not shrink at an allusion to it, as
though she feared to think of Sid, or would con-
sign him for ever to oblivion.

"It's almost time we heard how Sidney was,
father," she said.

"Ah! it is. His cousin said that we should
see him very shortly."

"It depends upon the doctor, I suppose," said
Mattie; "he has promised to obey Doctor Bario
implicitly."

"That's the reason, doubtless," said Mr. Gray: "well, I shall be glad to hear from him—a long silence between friends is always unsatisfactory, and often leads to unsatisfactory results. We shall hear from him very shortly, I feel certain. That young man, his cousin, might have called—I have much to tell him about his future course in life, if he will only listen to me. I mark progress in him, and he must not falter in the narrow way."

Mattie thought that Maurice Hinchford might have called more frequently if it had not been for the good advice that lay in wait for him, but she did not tell her father so. Her father meant well, and she seldom attacked his "best intentions." He was a man who had done much good—chiefly in a darker sphere than his own, where hard words are wanted for hard hearts—and she respected his opinions. She had not understood him very quickly—such men are always hard to understand —but she knew his genuineness, and it was not difficult to love him.

"What should I have done without him in this strait?" she often thought; and for his presence there—showing that there was some one to love, and some one who loved her—she was deeply grateful.

"Every day I expect visitors now," continued Mr. Gray, "and think it very singular that no one . calls. You will be glad to see Sidney, Mattie?"

"Very glad."

That same evening a letter arrived for Mr. Gray, informing him that the elders of his chapel would be very glad to see him on the following afternoon—a letter that turned the subject of discourse for that day, and took Mr. Gray away upon the next. During his absence the first visitor arrived.

Mattie was in the shop, when Maurice Hinchford entered, walked at once to his high chair, and assumed his customary position there. Remembering what had happened since then, Mattie winced somewhat.

"Good afternoon, Miss Gray," he said, shaking hands with her. "Given up for lost, and considered the most ungrateful of human kind, I am sure?"

" No, sir."

" To tell you the truth, we have had a bother with that cousin of mine. He's so horribly obstinate, we don't exactly know what to do with him."

" He's no worse ?" asked Mattie, eagerly.

" Worse!—he's so much better that we cannot keep him quiet. We locked him up a week in the dark, and then gave him light in homœopathic doses —globules of light, in fact—and so brought him round to a natural state of things. He is told to be cautions, and we catch him writing a letter to you, and we foil the attempt, and get sauced at for our pains. Then he wants to come back here directly, on business, he says; and we take him *nolens volens* to Red-Hill, and lock him up in our rooms there, with my sisters to see after him during our absence, and at length he is pacified a bit, and re-signed to country air."

" Have you come at his request, sir ?" asked Mattie.

" Yes. I promised faithfully to call to-day, and assure you that he is nearly well, and will shortly surprise you by a visit. He is very, very anxious to see old friends. That's my commission ; and now, Miss Gray, about this conspiracy of ours— will it succeed ?"

Mattie drew a long breath, and then prepared herself. She knew where his interest lay, and how unconscious he was whither her thoughts had drifted once, but she was prepared to meet all now. It was for every one's content, save hers. Only herself shut out from the general rejoicing in the cold ante-room wherein no warmth could steal !

" It will succeed, I think—I hope."

" Yes, but how are we to begin ?"

" Harriet Wesden and Sidney must meet and explain all that they have thought concerning each other—that's all."

" Ah ! that's all ! Quite enough, considering how difficult it is to bring them together. Difficult, but not impossible, Miss Gray ; we shall skim round to the proper method in due course. Harriet Wesden's appearance roused him, did it not ?"

" I think so. Has—has he ever spoken of it since ?"

" A very little—he's plaguey quiet on matters

in that quarter. He was very anxious to know what he said when he saw her, what she said, and you said; and after he had got all that *he* wanted, you might as well have tried to elicit confidence from an oyster. I try every day to bring the topic round, but he dances away from it, or curtly tells me to shut up. And now, may I ask a question?"

"If you will," said Mattie, a little nervously.

"What does Miss Wesden think?—you have seen her very frequently since the meeting at Doctor Bario's?"

"On the contrary, I have not seen her at all."

"Miss Gray! Miss Gray!" he said, reproachfully, "you are not working heart and soul with me! Here are two human beings who love each other, and will never be happy without each other, and we are letting time go by and harden them."

"I thought that Miss Wesden would have called here, and that we might have proceeded on *our* plan with less formality. But if she do not come shortly, I must visit her."

"Thank you—just sound her, if you can. She's a girl that will not be ashamed to own what impression the meeting with Sidney has made upon her; and after that, we'll set to work in earnest."

" I will write to her this evening, asking her to spend an hour with me."

" Ah! that's a good plan—looks better than calling. Now I will just tell you how we might manage to bring Sidney and her together—you're not busy?"

" No."

" Nor I. I have given myself the whole day to mature this plan, and if you consider it feasible, why we will carry it out, and chance the *dénouement.*"

He tilted his chair on to its front legs, and leaned across the counter to more closely impress Mattie with his logic; at the same instant the door opened, and Mr. Gray entered and gave him good day.

" Pleased to see you, Mr. Hinchford; you bring good news, I hope, of my absent partner?"

"The best of news, sir," answered Maurice; "your daughter will tell you how well he is progressing, and whither we have taken him.

You are at home for the day, I suppose, sir?"

"Yes—will you step into the parlour, and take a quiet cup of tea with us. We shall be proud of your company, and I shall be glad to have a little talk with you afterwards."

"Thank you, I have not dined yet, and—and I am very much pressed for time to-day, or nothing would have given me greater pleasure. Some other time, I hope, I shall be more fortunate. Please excuse this hasty visit, but business must be attended to—good-bye, sir—good-bye, Miss Gray —how late it is, to be sure!"

And backing and bowing politely, Maurice Hinchford reached the shop-door, darted through it, and dashed away from his tormentor.

"That young man is always in a terrible hurry," said Mr. Gray; "a good man of business, with a knowledge of the value of time, I daresay. Still he should not give up serious thoughts for thoughts of money-making entirely. I hope to find him more at his leisure shortly."

But Mr. Gray never did. Maurice Hinchford reformed, but it was after his own method, not

Mr. Gray's; and being a fair repentance, we need not cavil at it. He was ever truly sorry for that past, and all the wrong that he had done in it; he sobered down, fell in love once more, and in "real earnest;" married well, and made the best of husbands and fathers. The reader, who will meet with him no more on this little stage, whereon our characters are preparing to make their final bows, will I trust be glad to hear of Maurice Hinchford's better life, and to forgive him all his past iniquities. He has been the villain of our story; bad enough for real life, but in these latter days scarcely villain enough for the pages of a novel. Let us take him for what he is worth, and so dismiss him from our pages.

Father and daughter went into the parlour.

"Now let us hear all about Sidney," Mr. Gray said in the first place.

Mattie told him all that she knew, and he listened, rubbed his hands one over the other complacently, and exulted, like a good man as he was, over the well-doing of others. He indulged in a short prayer also for all the goodness and mercies vouchsafed to Sidney; and Mattie, who had never become reconciled to these sudden and spasmodic prayers, yet joined in this one with all her heart.

"Now," said he, suddenly assuming his every-day briskness, "for *my* news. But in the first place, don't excite yourself, Mattie—because it ends in nothing."

"Indeed!"

"I am not fond of exciting situations, and therefore I begin with the end, in order that I may not be excited myself. The end is, that I declined their offer, Mattie."

"What offer?"

"We'll come to that next. They wanted to see me at the chapel—there's a great scheme afoot for a further extension of the missionary project; they want a very energetic man for Africa—just such a man as I am," he added, with that old naive conceit which set well and conveniently upon him, because he spoke the truth after all; "and they've altered their opinion of that other man, who, if you remember, stepped into my shoes some time ago."

" Yes, I remember.".

" But they were too late—I told them so. I said
that though my daughter was about to marry and
have a home of her own, yet I had learned to love
her so dearly that I did not care, in my old age, as
it will be presently, to begin life afresh without
her. I thought that I could do my Master's service
here as elsewhere, and that I would rather give up
that good chance than give up you, and go away
for ever."

" For ever !—why ?"

" I was to settle down at the Cape—minister
at a chapel there that will be completed before
the next vessel arrives—and I felt too weak of purpose, Heaven forgive me, to leave you altogether."

" And you declined?"

" Yes, firmly and decisively. Perhaps it was
wrong."

" Go back, then, at once—don't lose a moment,
lest they should think of another man whom they
can put in your place !"

" What !—what !—what !" he cried, jealously,
" you wish to get rid of me like that."

"No—to go with you—share your life and labours there—be happy with you!"

"Mattie!—what does this mean?"

He held her at arm's length, and looked into her tear-dimmed eyes; he read the truth at last there, and, though unable to account for it, he folded his stricken daughter to his heart, and even wept with her. A man who had known little of earth's romance, or of the tenderness of life, and yet who understood it, now it was face to face with him, and could appreciate the loneliness of her whose life had become linked with his own.

"So," he said, at last, "you do not—you do not love Sidney well enough to become his wife?"

"Yes, I do. I love him too well ever to make him unhappy by becoming so, and standing between him and one he loves so much better than me. Some day I will tell you the whole story—explain it more minutely—you will spare me now, and keep my secret ever?"

"Ever," he responded.

"He will never know how I have loved him, therefore his memory will not be embittered by thinking that I—I felt this separation very much. I shall give. him up—that's all! I don't think that he will care for any explanation—and after that, I should very much like to go away with you to a new world."

"Beginning life anew, and leaving all old troubles behind us—well, if it must end like this, so much the better, Mattie!"

Mattie was silent for awhile, then said suddenly—

"You will go back now, and tell them that your daughter is anxious to go with you—to serve you there, and be your faithful servant in the good work lying before us both."

"If it's certain that you——"

"Father, there can be no alteration in *me*."

Mr. Gray took up his hat again and prepared to depart. He would have liked to attempt consolation to his daughter, but he felt, probably for the first time, that his efforts would have resulted in no good—that she was already resigned, and that the utterance of trite aphorisms would only unnecessarily wound her.

He departed, and Mattie, true to her old busi-

ness habits, took once more her place in the shop.
She was glad that there was no business doing
that afternoon—that Peckham in the aggregate was
undisturbed with thoughts of stationery. She
could sit there and deliberate upon her plans 'for
bringing Harriet and Sidney together—they must
be happy at least, and she must not go away from
England uncertain about their future. Two old
sweethearts, whose liking for each other had only
been temporarily disturbed—for whose happiness
she had made many efforts, and did not flinch at
this one. After all, she thought, their happiness would be hers—and she should go away content.

Then there rose before her that future for herself, and she could see in the new life, in the new
world, that which her father had prophesied. All
the old troubles would be left behind on the old
battle-ground ; she would make up her mind to
that, and thus life would be different with her, and
happiness for her, perhaps, follow in due course.
She had no idea of being unhappy all her life, because she had discovered that Sidney Hinchford's

heart had been true to its first love ; on the contrary, she was certain now that she should get over
all her romantic difficulties in a very little time.
At the bottom of all this was the woman's pride to
be above all petty sorrowing for those who had
never really loved her,—as she deserved to be
loved,—and that would keep her strong, she knew.

Afar, then, she saw herself happy enough in
the new world—with the familiar faces of her
father and Ann Packet to remind her of the old.
New friends, new pursuits, new incentives to do
good, and defeat evil at every turn of her life—
her young life still—with scope for energy and a
fair time given her, not entirely alone, and never
unloved, there would be nothing to disturb, and
much to gladden, the future progress of the stray.

When her father returned in the evening, he
found her very anxious to learn the result of his
second journey to London.

"Were you in time ?" she asked.

"Yes. It's all settled, my dear."

"I am very glad of that," she murmured; "there
is no uncertainty about our next step."

"No—we must see Sidney now, dissolve partnership, and put the shutters up, Mattie."

"We must write to him in a day or two about the partnership—I would prefer that they know nothing of our intentions until the last instant—until we are ready to go—perhaps until we *are* gone. I don't think I could stand up against all their good-byes and best wishes—I would rather go away quietly, with you and Ann."

"Ann!"

"We must not forget her."

"She'll never go to the Cape, my dear—she can't go to Finsbury to bank her wages without hysterics, now."

"Because she's nervous, and I don't go with her," said Mattie.

"Ah! I see—you're right, my child. Ann Packet will have no fear about accompanying *us*. And she'll make a much handier servant than a Zulu Kaffir."

"And we'll go away quietly," said Mattie again.

"Yes my dear, if you wish it. I object to anything in the dark, but as it's for your sake—I promise."

" Thank you," whispered Mattie.

Whilst Mattie was writing a letter to Harriet Wesden, as she had promised Maurice Hinchford—Mr. Gray broke the news to Ann Packet, and impressed secrecy upon her. Ann Packet was asked to state her wishes, and Mattie looked up from her desk and smiled at the old faithful servant.

" Anywhere's you like," said Ann, without a moment's hesitation; " black men or brown men— I suppose they're one or tother there—won't matter anythink to me. I'm too old to care about the colour on 'em. And, Miss Mattie"—she always called our heroine Miss Mattie in Mr. Gray's presence—" whilst you're at your desk, do'ee give notice at my bank about my money."

" Plenty of time, Ann," said Mr. Gray; " we shan't leave here for two months yet, at least."

" Then give 'em two months' notice," was Ann's rejoinder. " There's thirty-seven pounds nine and sevenpence halfpenny in there, and they may as

well be told to get it ready for me. If they've
been a speccilating with it, it'll give 'em time to
call it in."

CHAPTER VII.

RETURNED.

MATTIE dispatched her letter to Harriet that same evening; in her epistle she expressed surprise that they had not seen each other since the meeting at Dr. Bario's—should she visit her, or would Harriet walk over to Peckham to-morrow afternoon ? She would be entirely alone, her father had business in town to attend to, and she was very anxious to see her old friend.

Mr. Gray's business in town did not take him from home till twelve in the morning; prior to that he went to work at his stock. When he returned home, he would endeavour to write a few lines to Sidney Hinchford; and whilst he was thinking what he should say, and whilst, despite his efforts to keep these thoughts back, they would intrude upon his figures, and throw him out in his accounts, Sidney Hinchford himself walked into the shop and stood before the counter, waiting for his partner to look up.

Mr. Gray, unmindful of Sid's propinquity, still bent over the books on his counter, and scratched away with his pen; Sidney, with his glasses on—the old Sidney of Suffolk Street days —stood very erect and still, smiling to himself at the surprise he should create.

Mr. Gray looked up at last.

"God bless me!" he ejaculated, and swept pens, ink, and account books on to the floor in his amazement, "it is you, then!—it *must* be you!"

"It looks like me somewhat, I hope," said Sidney, laughing and extending his hand, which the other warmly shook.

"Yes," said Mr. Gray, "and what a time it is since we have seen you! We were beginning to think that you had quite forgotten us."

"I never forget my best friends," Sidney replied, "and you and Mattie are the best that ever

I have had. Did Mattie think that I was likely to forget her?"

" Well, not exactly," said Mr. Gray, " and if you'll wait a moment I'll run upstairs and call her——"

"No, you'll stay here," said Sidney, firmly; "don't disturb her on my account. I shall see her presently, and I want to enjoy the luxury of her surprise. Besides, there's no hurry."

" Isn't there?" Mr. Gray asked dreamily.

" Why should there be? I'm here for good."

Mr. Gray had just stooped to pick up his books and inkstand; he dropped them again at this, and then emerged like a phantom above the counter once more.

" You don't mean that?"

"This is my home again. *They* were very kind to me at Red-Hill, but it wasn't like home, and it never felt like home to me. After Maurice had left for London this morning, I told them my mind very plainly—it's no good telling that harum-scarum fellow anything—expressed my thanks, my gratitude for all that they had done for me, packed up and came away. I was unsettled, dissatisfied, unhappy, somehow—and here I am."

Mr. Gray sank behind the counter again, this time to hide his confusion, which, it was evident, was visibly expressed on his countenance. Sidney back again! Sidney, without preliminary warning, once more entering his home as a friend who expected to be heartily welcomed, and as a partner whom he had no right to ask to go away! Mr. Gray did not see his way very clearly to the end; Sidney's "straightforward" habit of doing things had completely discomfited him for the nonce. He must take his time, and think of this!

He re-emerged from his hiding-place, and laid the *débris* he had collected on the counter.

"I was taking stock when you came in, Sidney," he said; " just seeing what each share would be, and so on."

" Indeed ! what was that for ?"

" Why, you—you are going back to the bank again as clerk. I believe you promised that," said Mr. Gray.

" When my sight will allow me—that will be in

a month or two's time—I shall return to the old
life, God willing.   But what is that to do with
taking stock ?"

"We shall give up this partnership together, of
course."

"I don't see why," said Sidney; "I shall still
want a home after business-hours, and there is no
home but this that I shall ever care for.   The
business has not become so large an undertaking
that Mattie and you cannot manage it."

"No, it's not that."

"And when—when I am married, we can talk
about giving it up then, or making it over to you,
or anything you like," said Sidney—"and so we'll
dismiss the subject."

"For the present—we shall have to talk of it
again.   Mattie and I are tired of it, and have
thought of something new, Sidney.   But, we'll
explain all presently.   Mattie, I have no doubt,
would rather tell you herself."

Sidney looked surprised, even discomfited.   He
did not comprehend the hint which Mr. Gray had
thrown out; he did not entirely see the drift of

Mr. Gray's conversation, or understand very clearly what was the difference in his partner's manner, which rendered his return something more than an agreeable surprise. He thought that he had discovered the solution to the mystery, and said,

" Old friend, you are vexed at my long silence; you have been harassing yourself—perhaps Mattie and you together—about my anxiety to get away from here, after God has pleased to give me back my sight. And I have been struggling and scheming to get back, and escape the kindness of my relations! Why, Mr. Gray, this will not do —this is not like you to mistrust true friends, and think uncharitably of them after their backs are turned! You should have known me better, and have had more faith in me by this time."

"My dear Sidney," exclaimed Mr. Gray, "I have never had an uncharitable thought towards you. I knew that you would always think well of us—that—that you were not likely to forget us. Until yesterday, I have been building upon your return here, and thinking how happy we should all be together."

"Until yesterday—what happened yesterday?"

"Mattie will tell you, Sidney—I cannot—I must not."

"Very well, we will wait," said Sidney, gravely; "there is nothing she can tell me which I cannot explain away."

"Are you sure?" was the father's eager question.

"Sure," he answered; but there was something in the tone which wavered, and Mr. Gray fancied that he detected it. He said no more, however; he was glad to see Sidney disinclined to elicit further information. Sidney paced the shop once or twice, looked round it, and then went into the parlour, without waiting for Mr. Gray's invitation, and looked carefully and curiously round the room also.

Mr. Gray followed him.

"I see the home for the first time, if you remember," said Sidney; "here, in the darkness, a fair life was spent, thanks to you and *her*. Here you both first taught me that there was comfort even in affliction; and here stood by my side, and fought my battle, two dear friends. What has altered them?"

"Nothing has altered their love and esteem for you, Sidney," said Mr. Gray ; "whatever happens, you must believe that."

"And what has altered my love and esteem for them?" was the quick rejoinder.

"Nothing, I hope—I believe."

"Then let us settle down into our old positions here. I have come in search of peace and rest ; of the old comforts which my uncle's grandeur could not give me, and which by contrast only rendered me more restless. I find them here, or nowhere. I take my stand here and expect them, or the disappointment will be a bitter one. This is home !"

He took off his hat, and seated himself by the table—a home-like figure, which Mr. Gray felt was in its place again. He leaned his forehead on his hand, and looked down thoughtfully—an old position in his blindness, which Mr. Gray had often watched, and which drew again more forcibly the heart of the watcher towards him. That heart

might have been a little estranged since yester-
night; it had borne no malice, but it had thrilled a
little at his daughter's confession, and the thought
had crossed it that Sidney Hinchford might have
spared Mattie an avowal of such weak love as
had been borne towards her. Sid had guessed
Mattie's secret, perhaps, and taken pity upon
her; he was generous enough for that, but he had
forgotten that Mattie was not humble enough to
accept it. Mr. Gray could almost believe now that
all had been a mistake, which Sidney's presence
there would satisfactorily explain; and yet Sidney's thoughtfulness and restlessness forebade
it.

Sidney looked towards him suddenly.

"What are you thinking of?"

"Of the change in you, Sidney—and of the
home that it really looks again for a little while."

"For a little while," echoed Sidney; "oh! you
will not explain—call Mattie, then, and let us end
this. I always hated mystery," he added, a little
peevishly.

Before Mr. Gray could cross the room to fulfil

his partner's commands, the door opened. Mattie entered, and paused upon the threshold with her hands to her quickly-beating heart.

" Sidney here—-at last?" she faltered forth.

" Yes, at last," he said, advancing towards her ; " *at last*, as your father has said, and now you. I have returned to find that you have both lost confidence in me, and both misunderstood me cruelly."

" I hope not, Sidney."

They shook hands together, and looked one another long and steadily in the face.

" It is upwards of a year since I have seen you, Mattie. It is the same hopeful, earnest face, that I have ever known—can there be a difference in me ?"

" No, you are unchanged."

" You both thought that I had forgotten you ?"

" No."

" You must prove it by your old ways, then ; or I shall never think this place the dear home I left a month ago."

" You have come back to——"

" To stop ! Why not ?—don t you wish it ?"

"I—I will tell you presently—give me time, Sidney."

"I am in no hurry," he answered, coldly.

There *was* a difference then!—they were inclined to resent his long silence, by something more than a rebuke ; they would not understand that he had been kept away against his will, by his doctor's orders, and that he had been cautioned not to write or read, or test his sight more than he could help. They had not been satisfied with his messages sent by Maurice Hinchford ; they *had* mistrusted him ! It was all very strange, and intensely disheartening ; he could have trusted them all his life, and he had believed that their faith would last as long as his. Presently they would know him better, see that he had not wavered in one thought or purpose, which he had formed before his sight came back ; but the consciousness that they had formed an estimate unworthy of his character, would remain with him for ever, and no after-kindness, and fresh faith, would obliterate it from his memory. There was an anxious silence; then the father's and daughter's eyes met.

"I think that I'll run into the City now," he suggested, feebly. He scarcely liked to leave his daughter at this juncture; but he knew her strength, her power to explain, and her wish that he should go. It did not seem natural that he should leave her with that strange young man, and, after he had risen to withdraw, he hesitated again.

He went slowly into the shop, and Mattie followed him.

She had read his thoughts correctly, for she said at once—

"I shall not give way before him. I am firm and cool—feel my pulse, it does not throb more quickly because I have to tell him that I will not be his wife. Before you come back, it will be all over, and I shall be waiting for you—the calm, unmoved daughter, that you see me now!"

"There'll be no scene, then?"

"All commonplace, and matter of fact—I will have no scene," she said firmly.

"Then I'll go. God bless you, my child!—if I couldn't trust you implicitly, I wouldn't move a step."

He went away, and she returned to the parlour, where Sidney had been sitting, a watcher of this whispered conference.

"Now, Mattie," he said.

Mattie sat down a little distance from him, and their eyes met steadily once more, and flinched not.

"Now, Sidney!"

CHAPTER VIII.

"DECLINED WITH THANKS."

IT had come at last, that day of explanation. Mattie would not give way therein; she had long prepared for it, prayed for strength to sever all past ties, and leave him ignorant, if possible, of her real thoughts concerning him. Whatever happened, she would be firm, she thought; and now with Sidney before her, she did not feel that she should waver. An artificial strength it might be, but it would support her throughout that interview, whatever might be the re-action after he had passed from her sight, never to see her again, if she could hinder him.

Ann Packet, who had been out on divers errands, stepped into the shop at this juncture, marked the occupants of the parlour, and went immediately

behind the counter, to attend to business during
that interview, and confuse the accounts inextricably, supposing that there was any business likely to
drift that way just then.

Mattie and Sidney had the little room all to
themselves, and there was no likelihood of being
disturbed. "Now, Mattie"—"Now, Sidney," had
been said between them, and then each waited for
the next words—as a duellist might wait for the
sword's-point aimed at his heart.

Mattie spoke first.   It was evident that Sidney
Hinchford would have waited all day.

"A few days before you went away from here,
Sidney," said Mattie, "you asked me a question,
and I promised that in good time, and with due
consideration, I would reply to it. Do you wish
that question answered now ?"

"I have come for it," was the reply.

He knew by Mattie's manner what that answer
would be, and he steeled himself to meet a cold
rejection of his offer. All was part and parcel of
the new incomprehensibility upon which he had
intruded.

"More than once, Sidney, I have thought of writing my answer to you, but have found the difficulty of putting all I wish to say into words that would not look cold and indifferent to the great honour you would have done me."

"This is satire," he said, hastily.

"Forgive me, it is not intended for that. I would not wound you by a word, if I could help it. And it was an honour to *me*."

"I deny it," he answered, warmly.

"Ever before you and me that past which there is no shutting from us—which would have been talked about, and have often brought the blush of shame to your cheeks for my sake. Ever before you what I have been—what I am fit for!"

"Fit for a higher station than it is in my power to raise you—no position is too elevated for a good and pious woman. All this is argument which I thought that I had combated long since—pardon me for adding, all this foolish reasoning, utterly unworthy of you."

"Still——"

"It is no reason for declining my hand, Mattie,"
he interrupted, with some sternness, "it is simply
an excuse."

Mattie winced for an instant, then her quiet
voice, firm and even as the way she had chosen for
herself, replied to this—

"Let me proceed, Sidney. You will hear me
out fairly, I am sure."

"Why not say No at once?—you mean to tell
me that you do not care to be my wife, and share
my home. Is not that your answer?"

"Yes—but I cannot let you think that I have
been insensible to your offer, or not weighed it
carefully in my mind before I thought that it was
not right that I should marry you. Sidney, had it
pleased God never to have restored your sight, I
would have been your faithful wife, serving you as
I alone was able, perhaps, and rendering you content with me."

"I see. You would have taken pity on my
loneliness—with that strange idea of being grateful for past kindnesses of a trivial description, you
would have sacrificed your happiness in an attempt

to attain mine. Mattie, it would have been a terrible failure."

" No."

" I say a terrible failure, which would have embittered both lives in lieu of promoting the happiness of either. I should have discovered the motives which had placed you at my side, and felt too keenly the encumbrance that I was upon you."

"I think not!—I am sure not!"

She was anxious to defend herself, to hold her best in his estimation yet, but she feared the betrayal of her secret. She could have told him how, for a few fleeting days, she had pictured her greatest happiness to be ever near him, striving to brighten every thought, and vary the monotony of every hour—sustaining, comforting, and worshipping. She could have told him of the affection of a whole life that had been spent in thinking of him, praying for him ; but she held her peace, and let him think that she had never loved him. In the end, she saw that it was best to turn him from his purpose.

" I would have married you, Sidney, in affliction

—out of gratitude, if you choose to word it so, but a gratitude that *you* would have never known from love," she ventured to say; "but now, when the new life, to which you will shortly turn your steps, is far removed from mine, when you require no help from me, and when there are others, fairer, better, and so much more worthy of you, I cannot hold you to a promise of which you must repent."

"Why?"

The position by some means had become suddenly reversed. It was she who had to speak of his pity and gratitude for her.

"Because you would discover that I was not fit to be your wife, that you had not sought me out of love, but out of kindness towards me for my services. You had pledged your word in one estate, and you would keep it in another, like an honest man valuing a promise he had made, and resolving to go through with it to the end, at whatever cost to his own better chances. Therefore, Sidney, you must understand that I cannot be your wife for pity's sake—that the man who is to become my husband, must love me with all his heart, and soul, and strength, or he may go his way for me!"

"I said that my romance had died out long ago. That I was too old, and had experienced too much sorrow to talk like a lover in a novel."

"It seems to me—I do not know, Sid—that true love must belong partly to romance. It is too pure—too full of fancies, if you will—to mingle readily with business life; it is too deep down in the heart to rise to an every-day surface—it is full of sacrifice as well as love. All this, my idea, not yours, Sidney—I who would at least be romantic in that fashion, and would care for no one but a romantic lover."

"You have altered, Mattie—you are talking like a school-girl now. If that be another reason for refusing me, it is unworthy of you."

"It is another reason, for all that," replied Mattie; "let me dismiss it at once, if you are ashamed of it. You have come hither oppressed—burdened, I may say—with a sense of duty to me; let me raise the load from you by saying, that I will not be your wife. If I would have married you

even out of pity myself," she added, a little scornfully, "I will not take a man for a husband who
would have had pity upon me!"

"Very well," he answered, moodily.

"As your wife, never—but oh! Sidney, as the
old friend and sister, always! Don't think ill of
me because I cannot see my way to happiness—
don't think that there is any difference in me, or
that I value you less than I ever did. You understand me?"

"Scarcely, Mattie—you have altered very much."

"You must not think that—I have not altered
in any one respect—I would be ever your friend,
ever hold a place in your heart, ever be remembered as the poor girl who would have died to make
you happy!"

"But would not have married me for the same
purpose," answered Sidney, in a kinder tone; "is
that it, Mattie?"

"My marriage with you would have rendered
you wretched—don't deny it again, Sid—I am sure
of that!"

"Hence your answer. Well, if it must be, I will

rest content. I will believe that it is all for the best."

"Let me tell you another reason—the last—why I would not answer Yes to you. May I?"

"I am interested in every reason," he said.

"Because you were bound to another whom you loved once—*whom you love still.*"

He sprang to his feet, and then dropped back into his place, as though shot at by a pistol.

"Do you believe that I would come here with a mask on—a robber, and a liar?"

"Not intentionally, Sidney; because you have fought hard to keep the old love back, and to believe that it was gone for ever. You have fostered that idea by thinking uncharitably of *her*, by turning away from that true happiness which only marriage with her will ever bring to you. You are a man who has never changed; and in attempting to live down the past, have but more clearly discovered the secret of your life."

"What—what makes you think this?"

"I cannot explain it, but it is as true as that you and I will never marry one another for love, for gratitude, for anything," she answered. "Harriet Wesden and you should never have parted, but have understood each other better, and had more faith. You turned from her, and her pride kept her apart from you ; but, Sidney, through all, and before all, she holds that love still."

"I cannot believe that."

"Your cousin Maurice has told you so—now let me. You will never be happy without her—do justice to her, if you are the Sidney Hinchford whom I have ever known. Sidney, you *do* love her—are you not man enough to own it?"

"I love her as one who is dead to me—passed away out of my sphere of action, and never likely to cross it again!" he answered. "I have always thought so—I would have told you that these were my thoughts, had you asked me on that night I sought your hand. She was dead to me—gone from me—some one apart from the girl who lives and breathes in her place."

"That was romance—and that *was* love!" cried Mattie quickly; "for she was not dead, her love was not dead, and you were likely to meet in better faith at any moment unforeseen. Sidney, you *did* meet—you were affected by her visit, her evidence of the old tie still existent. Why deny this to me, to spare my feelings now! I am living for you and her,—I do not love you, but I am interested in your welfare, and anxious—oh! so anxious, Sid, to advance it."

" Harriet Wesden and I met under peculiar circumstances, that must have touched both hearts a little—all was over in an instant, like a lightning-flash, and here's the sober life again!"

" You *will* deceive yourself—until two lives are wholly blighted by your obduracy, you will go on asserting this dreamy theory, and believing in it."

" You are a strange girl—stranger and more incomprehensible to me than you have ever been, Mattie," he said wondering. " What can you think of me, that you coolly ask me to sit here and confess to a passion for another, after coming for an answer to a love-suit tendered you. By heaven! it is a mystery, or a dream!"

" When I was a little girl, untutored, and run

wild, I used to fancy that you two would marry;
when we shared the same house together, I saw
how fitting you both were for each other—how, in
your strength of mind and purpose, one weak woman would always find support and love. When
you were engaged, I felt a portion of your happiness, understood that you had chosen well, and
knew—knew how proud and happy she must be in
your affection! That was *my* dream—let it in the
end come true, for Harriet Wesden's sake, for yours
—even for the sake of the woman here at your side,
the sister and friend to tell you what is best."

"You are very kind, Mattie, but—but I cannot
own to anything. It is not fear, not shame—God
knows what it is, or what I am, or what I really
wish!" he exclaimed irritably.

"Leave it to me."

"No, for myself, my own battles. I will have
no woman's interference, no friend's advice. I
will go on to the end my own way."

"It is not ordered so. Look there—is this
chance which has brought her hither to-day, at this
hour?"

" Let me go away !" cried Sidney, starting to his feet.

Mattie, flushed and excited, caught him by the wrist; he could have wrested himself away from her grasp, but he would have hurt her in the effort, and a something in his own will held him spellbound there.

His sight was weak yet, and though he had guessed to whom Mattie alluded, he could but dimly distinguish a female figure advancing towards him, as from the mists of that past sphere of which he had spoken. It came towards him slowly, even falteringly at last; and he remained motionless, awaiting the end of all that might ensue on that strange day.

It was the past coming back to him, to make or mar him. He shivered as he thought of all the folly he had committed, if, after all, Mattie and Maurice were right, and even his own heart had misled him. He was a man whose judgment had been sound through life— why should he have erred so greatly in this instance ?

"Mattie—Mattie!" gasped Harriet, on entering, "what does this mean ?"

"That Sidney has been waiting for you," said Mattie, quickly, "to thank you for all past interest in him. Shake hands, you two, and let me—let me go away !"

"No, no, don't leave me, Mattie! You must remain. I have been ill. I—I am very weak."

"If you wish it, for a little while. You two are not enemies now—let me see you shake hands, then ?"

The old sweethearts shook hands together at Mattie's wish, and then stood shyly looking at each other, each too discomfited, even troubled, to say a word. Mattie had one more part to play before she could escape them.

CHAPTER IX.

MATTIE, MEDIATRIX.

HARRIET WESDEN was strangely afraid of the old lover—what he would say to her in the first moments of meeting, whether he would speak of the past in which she had been misjudged, of the present hour which had brought them face to face, or of the future for them both, and what it would be like from that day.

She was afraid to speak, afraid to trust herself with him, and she clung closer to the skirt of the old friend, a child still in moments of emergency, as she had ever been. Sidney Hinchford stood perplexed, amazed—what could he say in the presence of the woman to whom he had been talking about marriage?—what dared he say were she even to leave them to fight out their explanations their own way?

Mattie read the fear of one, and exaggerated in her imagination the reserve of the other; even then all might be marred, and all her efforts end in nothing, if she were not quick to act.

"I asked Sidney, as you entered, Harriet, if it were not something more than chance that brought you two together to-day—that brought him hither, in particular," she said; "I think it is—I trust that from to-day a brighter life opens for you both. Why should it not?—you who have kept so long asunder from each other, only require an honest mediator to pave the way for a fair explanation. Both of you will have faith in Mattie!"

Neither answered, but Mattie did not take silence for dissent.

"When Sidney was blind, Harriet, the thought did cross me once or twice that I had better marry him and save him from his utter loneliness—and I think that he was desperate, and would even have married me! When Sidney or I relate this story some day, we three shall have cause to laugh at it heartily, and think what a narrow escape we all have had—even I, who have never been able to understand Sidney like yourself—as you know! I have only seen, Harriet, that this Sidney of whom we are speaking has become a desperate man, soured by contact with himself, and full of vain regrets for much trouble that his own rashness has brought on him—that he wants one true friend to aid him now, more than ever he did!"

"Pardon me, Mattie, but you must not speak for me," said Sidney, blushing; "if I have injured Miss Wesden by any hasty action, I will explain it, and take my leave of her and you."

"You will explain of course," said Mattie; "and if you part again after that explanation, it will be your own faults, and I will never have confidence in either of you any more. For you two—both friends and benefactors, whose childish hands were first held out towards me—I must see happy; I have striven hard for it, and I hope not to find this last disappointment the keenest and the heaviest. Remember old days, and the old hope you had together in them."

"Mattie, you must be a very happy woman some day!" cried Sidney, "you think so much of making others happy."

"I hope I shall," said Mattie cheerfully—almost too cheerfully, save for those two pre-occupied ones from whom she hastened to withdraw. Harriet Wesden made no further movement to stay her; she sank into a chair, covered her face with her hands, and trembled very much; in her heart was a strange fluttering of fear and hope, and the struggle for pre-eminence was too much for her.

Yes, she was a weak woman—not strong and resolute, and with the will to conquer difficulties like Mattie; but still a woman very lovable and beautiful, and with a heart that was true enough to all who had been ever cherished therein. From the moment that she had understood it, it never swerved from Sidney Hinchford; it had known its greatest trial when Sidney turned away from her, sceptical as to the reality of any love for *him*.

She had doubted his love for her until that day when Mattie came to draw her into the old vortex, and then her faith in him came back, and life took fairer colours—she knew not wherefore, save that the reflex of that day's brightness might have shone upon her from the distance. For it was a bright day for both these old lovers; Mattie had augured well that one explanation—a few words, true and gentle, that scarcely stood for explanation even—would be sufficient, and disperse all clouds that had hung heavily above them. Both had had much time for thought and regret—both had found little solace on the paths of life they had pursued, and looked back very often at the life they had given up together.

But the worst was over, and the fairer time—the old love, almost, if that were possible—was coming back once more. Sidney had believed it, when Mattie had stolen into the shop and closed the door upon them; he had felt all his old love return at Harriet's appearance, at her fear of him; at her strange half-sad, half-reproachful look towards him when they had first met that day; he knew, then, how wrong he had been, and how rightfully Mattie had read him—what love he bore

to the weak girl still, and what a poor substitute
for love he would have offered the stronger, *better*
woman. Will our readers think that Mattie Gray
was worth a dozen Harriet Wesdens?—that Sidney
made a bad choice, and that the hero—if we dare
call him so—should have married the heroine according to established rule? Or will they believe,
with us, that he made his proper choice, and that
Harriet and he were the most fitting couple to live
happy ever afterwards? If he did not treat Mattie
as fairly as she should have been treated, it was an
error of judgment on his part, and we are all liable to errors of a similar description. He believed
that he was acting for the best; he had taught
himself in the first instance to believe in his love
for her, and when he had awakened to the truth
his honour would not let him draw back, until
Mattie's pride had released him. Later in life he
fancied, once or twice, that he caught a glimpse of
the real truth, but he kept the idea to himself, like
a sensible man; he had succeeded in life, and was
his cousin's partner then—perhaps more conceited
than in the old days. And if Mattie suffered for

awhile, why, heroines are born unto trouble, or where would be the subscribers to our story-books?

This was Mattie's great day of suffering—for ever to be remembered as a landmark standing out sharp and rugged in life's retrospect. No one ever guessed half the terrible battle which she fought that day; and how she came forth smiling and victorious, with the deep wounds hidden, lest her distress should affect others who were happier than she.

When she returned to that room again, they had forgotten her, as they had forgotten all the doubts, fears, jealousies, harsh words that had stood between them, preventing their reunion. They were lovers again, and were happy once more—for the first time, since he had taunted Harriet with pitying *him*, as Mattie had taunted him that very day!

Mattie forgave them—asked to be forgiven for intruding on their reverie, and bringing them back to thoughts of others sat down with them, and listened to their stories of what

their future was to be—to really be this time!—
and how, in their generous hearts, they had built a
plan for Mattie's share in it. They saw only
Mattie's effort to bring them together, nothing else,
in that hour; and they were very grateful, and not
selfish in their joy.

"To think it has all ended as you wished at
last—as you have prophesied it would end!"said
Harriet; "and to think that I even mistrusted
you at one time, and was cold towards you, who
sacrificed so much for me, in the old days."

"*In the old days!*" thought Mattie.

"It makes a great difference when one is
unhappy," said Harriet; "we look at things
sceptically, and are mistrustful of all good intentions."

"For awhile!" added Mattie.

"Ah! for awhile!" repeated Sidney, "for we
are three together now in heart, and there is no
mystery or misconception in the midst of us. For
ever after this—the sunshine!"

*   *   *   *   *   *

Sidney and Harriet were there when Mr. Gray

returned; they spoke of their reconciliation, and Mattie's share in it, and he listened very patiently, betraying but little animation at the recital. He was more anxious to speak of giving up the business, having other views, he said—and still more anxious to see Sidney, the young man whom he had loved like a son, and who had done such irreparable mischief, out of the house. He knew Mattie would have to endure more, if Sidney called that place home ever again; and Sidney, who thought of the natural embarrassments which would attend his further stay there, was ready to return to Red-Hill, and his uncle's home, after he had accompanied Harriet to her father's.

They were gone at last, and Mattie and her father were facing each other. Mattie's face was white, and her lip was quivering just a little as they went out together.

"Courage, Mattie," he said, "we shall not give way now. We have fought well, and the worst is over."

"Yes, the very worst!"

"You will not envy them their happiness—two

weak addlepated mortals, only fitted for each other. You will keep strong !"

"For ever after to-day. But you must not be too critical with me now that he is gone, and I have no longer any occasion to keep firm. Oh! father, I loved him very, very much!"

"It is hard to lose him, I know that," said he, as Mattie flung herself into his arms, and wept there.

"Harder to think that he never loved me after all!"

"Courage!" he repeated, "God knows what is best for you. He will bring you peace, I am sure!"

And in good time, when Mattie was young still, the peace of God, which passeth all understanding, rested on her, and rendered her content.

CHAPTER X.

CONCLUSION.

LINGER not, O novel-writer, at the helm when the ship sails into the harbour, or your readers will escape you. When the end is known, and the facts and fancies pieced together, remarks are wearisome. The lovers have made it up, and good fortune awaits them ; *bon voyage !*—what's the next story, who writes it, and is the heroine fair or dark, ugly or handsome? The readers are off to fresh leaves and pastures new, in much the same hurry as playhouse folk, who scent the conclusion and the tag, are scrambling over their seats whilst pater-familias is giving his blessing to the young couple, who haven't agreed very well till the last two minutes.

Who would care at this late stage for Mr. Wes-

den's surprise at his daughter's companion, or for
his delight at things "coming comfortably round?"
The end is known; there is no room for fresh
disasters—Sidney Hinchford marries Harriet Wesden, and there's an end of *that* book!

And yet there is another scene with which we
would fain conclude—those readers who are in no
hurry will be tolerant of our prolixity. It is a fair
picture, and we will very briefly sketch it whilst
our guests retire.

A scene on shipboard—the ship outward-bound
—the new minister and his daughter standing on
the deck, exchanging farewell greetings with visitors that have surprised them by their presence
there; Ann Packet, with her money sewed in her
stays, in the background. Two months have passed
since the events related in our last chapter—the
partnership has been dissolved, the business sold,
friends taken leave of in a very quiet manner
by Mattie, who knows that it is for ever, and
yet would deceive them all by an equable demeanour, and a talk of going away for a little
while.

The task is beyond her strength, and she betrays herself a little, and suggests doubts, which resolve themselves to certainties, and lead to this.

She is glad now that they have found out the truth; she would have spared herself a little pain, but lost a bright reminiscence—it is as well to say "Good-bye" honestly and fairly, and not steal away from them in the dark, and leave her name finally associated with a regret.

They are all there who have ever cared for Mattie, or been indebted to her. Sidney Hinchford and Harriet, and Harriet's father, very feeble now, and more inclined to stare over people's heads than ever. They are gently upbraiding Mattie for her vain deception, and speaking of the sorrow they feel at losing her. The tears are in Mattie's eyes, and she trembles and clings to the stout arm of her father, whilst she offers her excuses.

"I had not the courage to look you all steadily in the face and say that I was going away for ever —I preferred to see you all one by one, as though nothing was about to happen to separate us, and to leave to the letters, which are already in the

post-office, the last news which you have thus forestalled."

"You speaking of want of courage!" said Harriet.

"I am stronger now—I am glad now to see you
all—I can bear to say good-bye to you."

She says it well and stoutly, too, when the time
comes, and friends are warned to let the ship proceed upon its course, and not delay it by their presence there. With Sidney, facing him with her
hands in his, she gives way somewhat; she lets him
stoop and kiss her—for the second time in life—the
last!

"God bless you, Mattie!—best of women!" he
murmurs.

"God bless you, Sidney!—with this dear girl!"

She flings herself into Harriet's arms, and cries
there for a little while—there is no jealousy now—
Harriet is the little girl of old, old days, the first
of all these friends she has learned to love, and is
learning now to part with.

"To lose *you*, Mattie—the friend, sister, counsellor, whose good words and strong love have kept

me from sinking more than once—it *is* hard!"

"In a few months, a wiser, better, and more natural counsellor than I—trust in each other, and have no secrets—don't forget me!"

Thus they parted—thus hoping for the best, and believing that the best had come for all, Mattie is borne away to the new world, wherein her father had prophesied would come new friends, new happiness. And they came; for Mattie made no enemies in life, and won much love, and was rewarded for much labour in God's service, by that good return, even on earth, which renders labour sweet and profitable.

THE END.

www.ingramcontent.com/pod-product-compliance
Lightning Source LLC
Chambersburg PA
CBHW060526030726
47498CB00004B/1098